HUSTLE

HUSTLE

NIKKI FORTUNE

MYND
MATTERS

FIRST EDITION

Published by Mynd Matters Publishing
201 17th Street NW, Suite 300, Atlanta, GA 30363
www.myndmatterspublishing.com
Library of Congress Control Number: 2018903406
ISBN 978-1-948145-04-6 (pbk)
ISBN 978-1-948145-05-3 (hdcv)

Printed in the United States of America

This book is dedicated to my late Grandmother Ernestine Jefferson and Great Aunt Clara Johnson. Their resilience, determination, and Hustle to "make better lives" for our family will never be forgotten ... I love you, forever.

INTRODUCTION

"ROSIE! ROSIE! WHERE'S MY SOCKS GAL?" POPPA WAS hopping around on one foot like a chicken wit his head cut off. He couldn't do nuthin witout Ms. Rosie's help. He yelled, "Hurry up gal! I got to be gettin on up to the church early this morning. You and the chilren gone have to walk. Deacon Brown wanna go over the plans for the anniversary service."

Rosie walked over to the trunk and grabbed a fresh pair of socks as she rolled her eyes and handed them to Poppa. Ms. Rosie normally ain't ask Poppa too many questions. She mostly went along wit whatever he said. Something inside her musta not been sitting right. While she was standin over the wood stove stirrin the potato soup for suppa, she put her hand on her hip and asked real nasty, "So what y'all plannin on doin for the service?"

Poppa was puttin on his jacket while headin to the door. He turned around and yelled, "Gal, I don't know that's why we's having a meeting!" The door slammed behind him as he hurried to hitch up his horse and buggy.

Ms. Rosie watched him out the window as he took off down the road. Then she yelled up to Fanny, "Come

on here gal! Let's hurry and get up the road to church. We gots to walk this mornin cause your Poppa say he gots a meeting. Run get the little ones ready so we can reach church by preachin time."

Then, she yelled up to me, "Hamilton, you and Amos come on down here. Time to get on up to the church.

I answered, "Yes ma'am, comin'!"

She ain't knowed that I was listenin to her and Poppa all mornin. I heard her say, "Ernest think I'm a fool. Ain't no meetin takin place before no service. Them meetings is always after service!"

She turned the wood over in the stove to make the flame low while we was gone so nuthin would catch fire. She was a good lady. The girls and me really did love Ms. Rosie and I hated the way Poppa treated her. He treated her much like he treated us chilren, sometimes worse.

CHAPTER 1

Meet Ernest Fortune, My Poppa

POPPA BUILT OUR HOUSE BACK IN 1902. IT HAD THREE ROOMS FOR sleepin upstairs for us chilren, one room downstairs where Momma and Poppa slept, and a room wit a wood-burning stove that we used for heatin and cookin. We ain't have no runnin water or plummin so we got our water from a well. We also had an outhouse out back where we did our business. We was lucky if we got a bath once a month, usually when Momma couldn't take the smell no more! We ain't have no money for furniture so we had a couple of chairs, a rockin' chair, and a chess that we kept our clothes in. We was dirt poor, as the old folks would say. Momma used to make clothes for us out of potato sacks once the potatoes was finished. We would stuff hay in old feedbags for sleeping. Sometimes if we was out in the field workin or playin and we had to do number two, we'd find an old cornstalk to wipe our butts. Most of our meals had some kind of potatoes, and maybe some chicken or hog if we was lucky. Momma could really cook and she would cook them potatoes up a lot of different ways. We really loved her cookin!

Before Poppa married Ms. Rosie and had my half-sistas and brother, he was married to my Momma, Elna Fortune. They had six chilren together, me (Hamilton), Fanny, Gladys,

Mally, Amos, and Betty. I was the oldest and I helped wit all the young ones. Fanny came after me and she was Poppa's favorite cause she looked just like him, tall and thin wit a long head. She was mean just like him too! Fanny was a quiet gal that mostly stayed to herself but if you messed wit her, she'd tear fire to you. Everybody in Hustle knew not to mess wit her or none of us cause it would be hell to pay. One day after school, I got into a fight wit Wallace Mitchell. He was Ovetta Mitchell's son and liked pickin on us younger chilren. When he came up to me and tried to hit me, Fanny pushed me out the way and went to whalin on him. When she was done, he had a big ole black eye and went runnin on down the road. All the chilren was laughin at him. When his Momma came to the house and found out that Fanny had whooped him, she started whoopin him all the way up the road for lettin a girl beat him like that. We all had a good time laughin at them.

Gladys and Mally was nine months apart in age but most people thought they was twins cause they looked just alike and was always together. They was pretty brown skin gals wit long, thick brownish-red hair that they aint never like getting combed. Momma would send me to look all over the farm for them when it was time to get they hair did cause they'd always run off and hide. When I did find them, Momma would have to hold them down between her legs and they be hollerin like somebody was killin em. My baby brotha Amos was a little ole scrawny

boy and was always sick. He always had a cold or a fever. Seemed like he was sick more than he was well. He didn't bother much wit us other chilren and was always up under Momma's apron. He was a right nice lookin little fella wit the biggest brown eyes I ever seen, but there was always sadness in his eyes. I always felt right sorry for him and would try to make him laugh any chance I got.

Poppa and Momma was married for fifteen years when she died giving birth to my baby sista Betty. I remember when she was being born. It was a house full of folks waiting for the baby to come when Ms. Lattie bust out the room screamin, "Help! She done went cold! Help! Get me some rags! She bleedin bad! Somebody run and fetch Dr. Berger. Things ain't looking good for Elna! Somethin real bad done happened!" Ms. Lattie was sweatin and lookin scared. Then, she ran back in the room with Momma.

When she left, the room got quiet. Nobody was expectin to hear that, so everybody was frozen! Poppa looked like he was a ghost. I never seen a brown man turn white! Momma's sistas was even quiet for the first time ever. I was looking around at everybody when what all she'd said hit me. I jumped up and yelled, "I'mma go on and fetch the doctor! Poppa, stay here with Momma! Fanny, Mally, and Gladys, get some rags for Ms. Lattie and boil some more water! I'll be back as quick as I can!"

The girls ran off to start gathering rags and getting the water on when Ms. Lattie came out the room wit a lil

baby wrapped in a cloth. You could tell by the look on her face that something wasn't right.

She walked over to Poppa and almost whisperin said, "Elna gone. She gone on to be with the Lord. She in a better place." She handed the baby to Poppa with tears rolling down her face and said, "But you's got a new baby girl that's doin just fine."

When Poppa heard those words, he looked down at the baby then back up at Ms. Lattie before gettin up, walkin out the house, and slammin the door. All you could hear was wailin. Reminded me of what it sound like when a coyote get caught in a trap out in the woods. You could hear him hollerin for miles.

By now, everybody was cryin and carryin on. My Momma's sistas was almost faintin. One was no better than the other, fallin down and yellin. They was a mess! All of Poppa's friends and family that was over to the house was cryin too. My Momma was the baby girl of all her sistas and everybody loved her. I looked at Ms. Lattie and she was cryin, holdin, and rockin the baby back and forth. I ain't never heard that nobody died on Ms. Lattie watch, so I know she gots to be hurtin bad too. I went over and asked if I could hold the baby. Ms. Lattie knew that I knew what I was doin wit a new baby from all the babies in my family, so she gave her to me. She was a pretty lil thang and ain't had a clue about what just happened.

I rocked her and whispered in her ear, "Momma said

your name gonna be Betty. She ain't here no more but we's gonna be alright! I'm your big brother Hamilton and I ain't gonna let nuthin happen to you."

My younger sistas heard what Ms. Lattie said and they was just a hollerin and yellin. I went over to where they was sittin and said, "Y'all stop all that cryin. This here is y'alls new baby sista, Betty, and if y'all don't stop cryin, she gonna be afraid of you!"

They looked up at me and started dryin up they tears. For the time, they was playing wit they new baby sista and not thinkin about how our Momma was gone.

Everybody had calmed down and it seemed like hours had passed by before anyone said a word. The girls and me was still tending to the baby. Poppa was back in the house, looking out the window. He still ain't hold Betty yet. I guess the pain was too deep. Momma's body was still in the room waiting for the deacons to pick her up and take her to the church. Then, out of nowhere Poppa said, "Now y'all chilren listen up. Y'all Momma done gone to be wit the Lord. She was a good woman but she gone now and we all is gonna have to get use to it. That's the way the good Lord want it to be. If y'all want to, you can go on in the room and pay your respects to your Momma before the deacons come to get her body."

Once he finished talkin, he hung his head and walked back outside. All we heard was that same wailin sound from before. I was very close to my Momma so to hear Poppa say them words felt like somebody had ripped my

heart out my chest. I felt like I couldn't breathe! My sistas and Amos started cryin all over again and now Betty was hollerin too. My aunties tried to comfort us chilren but all I wanted was my Momma! I waited about five minutes while I was building up my nerve to go in that room. I ain't know what to expect. Ms. Lattie had said it was a lot of blood but it just wouldn't feel right to not say bye to my Momma. So, I walked over to Momma and Poppa's room door real, real slow. Even though it was hot like fire in the house, the knob felt cold as ice. I turned it real slow and cracked the door open. Everybody was still carryin on so they paid me no mind. I closed my eyes and pushed the door open. I leaned around the door still keepin my eyes closed. I counted to three and then I opened my eyes and my Momma was lyin on that bed looking like what I thought an angel would look like. I ain't see no blood nowhere. Ms. Lattie had cleaned her up and had her lyin in the bed on her back like she was sleepin. Her hands was folded over a little white Bible that was sittin on her stomach. She looked peaceful.

I went in and closed the door behind me. I walked over to the bed and put my hand on top of her hand. I pulled my hand back real fast because she was so cold and I was shocked. My Momma was a warm-blooded woman, so every time you touched her, you felt her heat. I walked around the bed and looked her all over. I wanted to rememba her in all her glory. Then, I whispered in her ear, "You was a good Momma. I don't know how we's

gone get along witout you but I promise before God, I will be a good man and make you proud. I'm gonna take care of these chilren and Poppa as long as it's life in me. You rest now and be happy with the Lord. I love you Momma." Tears was rollin down my face cause I was gonna miss my Momma!

Word start gettin round Hustle that my Momma had gone home to be wit the Lord and peoples was coming by and droppin off preserves and bread. Some people even fried a few pieces of chicken cause they knowed the family was gone need some help gettin on our feet again. Poppa ain't have no clue what to do wit us chilren, he was hardly ever home when Momma was livin.

My Momma's sistas and Mrs. Waller, from the church, was making all the funeral plans. Momma's funeral was gonna be the next week and everythang just seem like it was movin so fast. Just last week, we was happy and gettin ready for Betty to come and now we's buryin Momma. The house was quiet and felt empty the whole week. It was a sadness that I ain't never felt before and never want to feel again. My aunties came by a few times to check on us, but tendin to all us chilren was a lot of work and they had chilren of they own. They made sure we had somethin decent to wear to pay our respects to our Momma, and my Aunt Shirley braided up the girls' hair. But I felt so lonely, like we was on our own.

The day of the funeral, all the peoples from Hustle came out to show they respect for my Momma. People

even came from other counties to pay they respect. Reverend Waller said some mighty kind words about Momma. Everybody that said somethin talked about her nice heart, sweet smile, and how she could sang and cook! My sistas ain't do well during the service. They cried and hollered the whole time. Me, well I just held onto my baby brother Amos. A few tears fell down my face but I had to be strong for my sistas. Poppa sat there and ain't shed one tear. It ain't look good for a man to be cryin in front of all them folk, make him look weak.

After we buried Momma, everybody came back to the house to eat and talk. It was the way folks did to remember the dead. Emma Fortune was my Poppa's second cousin, but rumor had it that they was more than just cousins. When her and her chilren showed up at the house, people started whispering. She came wit a cake and gave it to Poppa. Her gals started playing with Mally and them and everybody was just lookin at her. She could tell that people was looking and wondering what in the world was she doin here.

That's when she said in a real sassy way, "Good day everybody! I come to offer my sympathy on the passin of Elna just like everybody else!"

Some peoples was about to speak when my Aunt Bonnie jumped up and said, "Emma, what you done come around this house sniffin for? It's one thing to show up at the church, but you know you up to no good when my sista ain't cold in the ground and you around here after

her man! You ain't here to offer no sympathy! Everybody know you and Ernest been f**kin for years and y'all is cousins! Don't bring yourself around here disrespecting the dead and her chilren in her house!"

By this time, all four of my aunties was standing behind my Aunt Bonnie and everybody else was staring at Emma and shaking they head.

Emma jumped up all red in the face. She yelled for her chilren, "Come on here y'all! Let's go! We ain't welcome here!"

She knew that was best cause she ain't want no parts of my aunties. So she and her chilren went stormin off down the road. They left so fast, dust was kickin up behind them! Poppa stood up and said, "Now wait a minute Bonnie. You don't come up in here the day I bury my wife makin claims about what I'm doin. You ain't the pillow nor the post and ain't never seen me f**kin nobody! Anyone of y'all havin thoughts about Emma and me can kiss my black ass and get on up out my house! I ain't never asked none of you for a thang and I gots no plans to!"

Once Poppa said that, everybody started gettin up and leavin. All the peoples was whispering about what my Aunt Bonnie had said to Emma. My aunties was fussing about the nerve Emma had to show up to the house. This ain't how I wanted my Momma's home going to be remembered. It felt like somebody had kicked me in the gut.

CHAPTER 2

Pickin Up After Momma Died

TEN MONTHS WENT BY AND THE FAMILY WAS STARTIN TO get along. Poppa ain't let nobody go to school no more cause there was too much work to do around the farm. We all had chores like cookin, cleanin, and taking care of Betty and Amos, and everybody had to help out. I spent my days and nights on the farm wit Poppa. We had to make sure we had a good harvest to feed the family and get through them long winters.

Being out on the farm all day wit Poppa, I could tell he was missin Momma. He'd stare off into the day and then I'd see a tear roll down his face. Ever since Momma died, Poppa had been stayin home at night and not hangin out wit his buddies or his lady friends like he used to. I think this had some of them womens goin crazy cause a couple times they showed up at the farm wit a cake or some biscuits just to see him. Poppa would send them off and tell them not to come back by the farm. I'd keep on workin like I ain't seen nuthin! But I reckon, spendin all his time just being around us chilren was startin to get to him, cause he started goin down and hangin at the juke

joint again.

Now, Poppa was a lady's man! Ever since I was small, him and Momma was always fightin about him runnin wit other womens. Nosey womens was always comin by the farm, specially my Momma's sistas. They would tell her how Poppa was foolin around wit cousins, friends, white womens, and anything wit a tail in Hustle. Poppa wasn't hard on the eyes neither. He was brown skin, tall, thin build wit muscles and black wavy hair. The womens from town loved him and would do anything to get on that farm and help him raise us chilren. One day, my aunties came by the house to get on Poppa for messin around wit Essie May. They said Robert Holmes was in the juke joint one night when Poppa came in and he told them everything that happened. Robert told my aunties that all the women start whispering and fixin theyselves up and spreadin the word that he was there. He told them that one girl had the nerve to say loud enough for everybody to hear, "You know he probably lookin for a wife, he need help with them chilren." All the women started chuckling and was giving him that look that say wit they eyes that they wanted to take care of his needs. Then, they said Essie May walked over to him and placed her hand on his waist and slid it down to his man parts and asked him what he was looking for in the juke joint? He said Poppa laughed and said, "Whatever anybody wants to give me. But I was hoping to start wit a drink." Then he smiled, moved her hand, and winked at her.

Essie smirked and walked around him runnin her hands cross his man parts again until finally puttin her hand on his chest. She told him that she had somethin for him, but she couldn't give it to him inside, he had to meet her out back. She switched off and turned around and used her finger to tell him to follow her. They said she ain't have no shame while she walked out the back door. (Now, I knowed Essie May from church and she was light skin wit long, pretty hair and had the biggest ass, thighs, and titties I ever seen and I was only thirteen! All the boys my age talked about what they wanted to do to her. We would see all the grown men in church lookin at her too when she would put her money in the collection plate. Everythang on her just bounce so nice!)

Robert told them that Poppa ordered him a whiskey, downed it, and went on out back to see what Essie May had to give him. I ain't understand why Robert followed them out back, but he did and then went and told my aunties everythang. When Poppa got close, Essie was leaning on the back of his buggy. He walked over to her and said, "Now gal, what you gots to give me?"

Essie May pulled him close and grabbed his d**k again and told him, "I have this nice, sweet, pu**y to give you. I been wantin a piece of you since I was fifteen years old and now that you is free and single, I want to see what all these ladies fussin about!"

She start kissing Poppa and they said Poppa pulled her dress up, pulled her panties down, and thrust himself

in her right there outside the juke joint! My aunties said that Robert Holmes seen them wit his own eyes!

They was actin like wild animals. They was on the ground and on the buggy. He was on top of her, then she was on top of him, and both of them was butt naked rollin around in the grass. He said when they was finished, Poppa start puttin his clothes on.

While Essie May was puttin on her clothes, she said to him, "Ernest, I knows you needs some help tendin to that house and raising all them chilren. I just want you to know that if you's lookin for somebody, I'm good with cookin, cleanin, raisin children, and takin care of a man and his needs."

He said Poppa started laughin and told her, "You knows how to take care of a man's needs, I'll give you that. But don't no man want no woman that he can have in the back of the juke joint raising his babies!"

Robert told them that Essie May jumped up and start fixin herself up and told him, "Ernest Fortune, you is a no good dog! I ain't the first woman that you done had in the back of a buggy and I won't be the last! Maybe you waitin for your cousin Emma Fortune husband to die so you can be wit her since you like f**kin your family!" She walked off and turned around and said, "You ain't never gonna get this sweet pu**y again!"

He said Poppa chuckled again and fixed his pants. When he went back in the juke joint, all the women was givin him the cold shoulder now cause they knowed

that he was out back wit Essie May. Poppa had another whiskey and left.

Poppa let my aunties finish and told them, "Yes, that did happen and I'm a single man and can f**k anybody I want to!" Then he told them to leave and don't come back. They called Poppa every name under the sun except a chile of God as they was walking down the road.

About three weeks passed since my aunties had came out to the farm. Me and Poppa was workin in the field when this horse and buggy was comin fast down the road. We couldn't see who it was cause it was kickin up so much dust. When the buggy got closer, we saw it was Jim Baker, the man who ran the town post office, and he ain't look happy. He was crackin the whip on them horses like crazy! As he got even closer, Poppa started walking towards him. He took his hat off and wiped the sweat off his forehead.

When the buggy came to a stop, Poppa walked over and said, "Jim, what brings you all the way out here?"

Jim looked mad cause he was red as a firecracker. "Nigger, you know why I'm here! Everyone in town knows that you been f**kin my wife Millie! I'm going to hang your black nigger ass!"

Poppa started, "Hold on a minute Jim! Now you can't be listenin to no town rumors-"

Before Poppa could finish, Jim cut him off and said, "If I hear it again, me and the KKK will be back here so fast and you and all those pickaninnies up in that shack will be burnt up like black coal! You can run around all

over town with all the nigger gals you want, but don't cross the line!"

Jim rode off like a mad man. The wheels on his buggy looked like they was gone roll off! I didn't say nuthin' cause Poppa was red in the face and looked real mad, he never liked being threatened. The rest of the day, we finished tending to the farm but we ain't say a word. I ain't never say nuthin' about what happened and neither did he.

When Sunday came, Poppa couldn't wait to go to church. As much as he tried to hide that Jim Baker coming out to the farm messed wit his head, I knew it did. He made the girls and Amos stay in the house all week and I couldn't go into town to run the errands like before. He even started sleepin in the chair wit the rifle right by his side. Poppa was usually a mild-mannered man except when he was drinkin but since momma died he wasn't even doin that so much.

Once the girls was ready, we all piled in the buggy and went up the road to Sunday mornin service. This Sunday was special, we had a church comin from Caroline County. Everybody was gonna be at Mt. Olive Baptist Church today. They was even havin fried chicken dinners for sale after service. All the folks would be sitting around in the picnic area eatin and singin. Our Momma always looked forward to Sundays, she used to be the best solo singer from Hustle. I sure did miss Momma and everybody else did too, but we was gettin along.

When we finally got to the church, there was at least fifty horse and buggies parked and about thirty peoples walkin up the road from all directions. A lot of women was speaking to Poppa and lookin at him, but ever since ole Jim came to the farm, Poppa ain't been much carin about no woman. He had been puttin in a lot of work around the farm and fixin up the house. He ain't never been around us chilren this much when Momma was livin. Anyway, we all headed in the church to hear Reverend Waller's preachin and the visitin choir from Mt. Zion Baptist Church. Everybody knew this church could sing. They had a piano player, drummer, and tambourines. Everybody in the church was singin, "Soon and very soon, we is goin to see the King." People was hollerin and jumpin up and down like they was at the juke joint! For a minute, I even saw Poppa havin a good time.

After service, we all went out to the picnic area. The girls was runnin around playin wit the other children. Poppa was talkin to some of the deacons and the Pastor was greetin the visitin guest. The sun was out and the sky was clear and blue. It was a real nice day for a picnic. Perched on a tree not too far away was a red robin just singin it's heart out. I even saw two butterflies playin wit each other and flyin all around us. It was a nice Virginia Sunday and all I could think about is how I wished my Momma was here. I thought about how she woulda been one of the womens that cooked up the chicken and how she would

do the girls' hair all nice and pretty. She would make sure that our Sunday best was clean because Momma never let us chilren go out looking as poor as we really was. She'd always add a little grease to our cocoa skin so we ain't look gray and ashy. By the time we reached wherever we was going, it was so much dirt and bugs stickin to the grease on us that we still looked just as dirty as the rest of the chilren. Momma ain't care about that. She knew how she sent us out and that was all that mattered to her.

When I finished daydreamin and looked up, I seen that Poppa was talking to a nice lookin young lady from the visiting choir. I hadn't seen Poppa smile in over a year and now he was smilin like a chessy cat. I ain't know what to think cause she ain't look that much older than me. That's how it was, the older mens always liked the young girls. This lady had pretty brown skin with long, silky hair and a real nice shape. I asked my cousin Sara from Caroline County who she was, she said her name is Rosie and that her momma was Indian and her daddy was a white man from King and Queen County. All I knew is all the mens was lookin her way. Just then I heard Poppa yell, "Boy, go and round up your sistas and come here. There's somebody I want y'all to meet!"

I said, "Yes sir," and went to find them girls.

When I found them, they was playing with Ms. Estelle's girls.

"Y'all come on! Poppa want y'all to meet somebody!" Fanny said, "Who he want us to meet?"

I told her that I seen him talkin to one of the choir singers from Caroline County.

She said, "Why we gots to meet her for?"

I said, "I don't know but don't go over there being all sassy before Poppa make you get a switch off the tree when we get back down the road!" Soon as I said that, they all straightened up.

When we got over to them, Poppa said, "Chilren, I'd like y'all to meet Ms. Rosie. She from Caroline County."

We said, "Hi."

Then in a nice, warm, lovin voice she said, "It sure is nice to meet y'all chilrens." Then she turned to Poppa and said, "You sure do have some beautiful chilren."

Poppa nodded with a proud look and said, "Thank you and they is good children. Ain't never gave me one day of trouble since they Momma died."

Ms. Rosie looked like she felt bad for us. She said, "Well, fine lookin chilren like these ain't gots no troubles in they bones. She smiled and said, "Let's get some of this chicken before it's all gone." We all smiled back and headed for a table.

Poppa and Ms. Rosie talked all afternoon. It was like they was the only ones at the picnic. They ain't talk to no one else the whole day. The girls and me played with the other chilren but I couldn't take my eyes off Poppa. I hadn't seen him smile so much in all my life. I ain't even knowed he had nice, straight teeth 'til then. After everyone had left, me, Poppa, and some of the other deacons stayed

to clean up. Poppa was hummin and movin like he was a new man. I kept trippin and runnin into stuff lookin at him. All the way home I stared at him out the corner of my eye cause it was something different goin on.

All that week, Poppa was actin the same way he had at the picnic. He was gettin up early and workin hard on the farm. Even when he came in all tired, he was still hummin and smilin. On Saturday evenin, he told us that he was going out to see Ms. Rosie. He washed up real nice, shaved, and slicked his hair down wit the Dax grease. He took out his Sunday outfit again and shined up his boots. He had washed the horse and buggy earlier in the day and I thought he was getting it ready for church, but he was gettin it ready to go see Ms. Rosie. Deep down, I was happy for Poppa. I ain't seen him this happy since the day Momma start having pains when she was birthin Betty. He was so happy that day and later that night I saw a sadness that ain't never went away...until last Sunday when he met Ms. Rosie.

Every Saturday for the next two months, Poppa would get all dressed up and have me watch the chilren while he was out wit Ms. Rosie. Ms. Rosie even start comin to our church and one Sunday after church, she came back to the house and cooked us a real nice dinner. We was all happy cause we ain't had a good, home-cooked meal since Momma died. She took a real liking to Amos and he liked her too, he was even smiling' and playin wit her. This made me happy cause since Momma died, he

ain't smiled not one time. Ms. Rosie even did all the girls' hair and for the first time ever, Mally and Gladys ain't run and hide. They actually let Ms. Rosie braid they hair.

It only took Poppa four months to marry Ms. Rosie and move her in and she became our new Momma. But for me, no one could take the place of my Momma so I always called her Ms. Rosie. The girls called her Momma Rosie. She was nice to us chilren and I was happy that Poppa found a wife. I was gettin tired of having to care after all those girls. I made them swear that they better never tell folks that I combed they hair since that was not somethin I was proud of. But I had to help Poppa out anyway I could.

When Ms. Rosie moved in, a lot of my Momma's family wasn't happy. My aunties came over to the house again and Aunt Vickie asked Poppa, "What is you doing having a chile raising Elna's children? She ain't but six years older than your son Hamilton?"

Ms. Rosie never said a word. Poppa told all three of them, "Yall ain't got no business meddlin over here in my affairs. I ain't seen none of y'all come by here to check on these chilren. You ain't combed not one of these gals' heads since your sistas funeral or asked if any of them was hungry! So don't come over here wit your nosey ass selves worryin on how I'm doing thangs!

Your sista is dead and gone! I was good to her while she was here but she ain't here no more. I gots to do what

I gots to do to make a family for these here chilren. Rosie and me is married and we gonna raise our family. Don't come round here starting no mess cause this is my wife and y'all gonna respect her. I don't care if she ain't but 18!"

He opened the door and my aunties rolled they eyes at Ms. Rosie right before they stormed out.

Poppa slammed the door behind them and he looked at us and said, "We is a family!" He went to the window and watched them walk on up the road. He was getting real tired of my aunties meddlin in his business.

In three months, Ms. Rosie was pregnant with her first chile. Everything seemed to be going good. Poppa was happy and not hanging out at the juke joint. All those late night buggy rides had stopped. The girls seemed to be liking having a Momma around again and me, well, I just liked that my family was okay and we could go to school a couple of days a week. As Ms. Rosie was getting bigger and bigger, us chilren was getting more excited. The girls wanted another girl of course, but I really wanted another brother.

Months had gone by until one day the girls and me was coming home from school and we could hear Ms. Rosie hollerin. We start running cause we knew she was having the baby.

When we reached the door, Ms. Estelle was blocking it, sayin, "Y'all chilren run and play. Rosie giving birth and need peace!"

Ms. Estelle was the new mid wife. After Momma

died, Ms. Lattie never birthed another chile. They say that losing my Momma cut her deep and she couldn't handle that it happened on her watch.

We was so excited we just sat down on the steps quiet as church mice. About five minutes had passed and out of nowhere, Amos start yellin, "I don't want Ms. Rosie to have no baby! I don't want her to die like Momma!"

He was crying so hard that Poppa had to come outside to see what was going on.

He opened the door and said, "Amos, why is you hollerin and screamin like a black snake done got to you?"

"I don't want Ms. Rosie to die like Momma!"

I saw all the blood leave Poppa's face cause it was like he was thinkin about when Momma died birthin Betty and now it was in his mind all over again.

I was shocked for a minute cause Amos was a little ole thing when Momma died and nobody even knew that he remembered what happened.

Poppa came outside, picked Amos up and said, "Ms. Rosie ain't gone die. God is a merciful God and wouldn't allow that to happen to Momma Rosie!"

Amos stopped cryin and hugged Poppa's neck. It was like Poppa was making hisself believe that and praying to God at the same time. Just then, we heard the cry of a brand new baby. Poppa put Amos down and rushed back into the house. When he came back to the door, he had our baby sista in his arms. He told us Ms. Rosie was fine and she was in the house restin. After rememberin what

happened to Momma, I ain't even care that I had another sista. I was just happy Ms. Rosie was okay.

Clara was the whitest colored baby I had ever seen and her eyes were blue like the sky. We ain't seen too many babies that looked like her that wasn't rumored to be some white man's baby. And believe me, there was gonna be a lot of folks talkin about it around town but no one would dare say nothin to Poppa. Besides, people said that Ms. Rosie was part Indian and white so the baby could look like her kin. There was a lot of black gals that had babies wit white mens in these parts. Them white mens loved black girls more than than they own kind and them white womens loved the black men too, but they act like they hate us.

Once Clara was up and walking, Ms. Rosie was pregnant again. I knowed I was going to get my brother this time around but Ms. Rosie had another girl and they named her Cicely. She looked more like what people expected a baby to look like comin from Poppa and Ms. Rosie. She was a brown little round baby wit big curly hair and blue eyes.

Our family was growin but so was Poppa's old ways. He was back hangin at the Juke Joint all the time. They say he was sleepin with his cousin Emma Fortune again too. Rumor was that the white woman that owned the sawmill had a thing for him too. Poppa was drinkin more and more and becomin very mean to us chilren and Ms. Rosie.

CHAPTER 3

Back To The Intro

AMOS AND ME WAS SITTIN OUT ON THE PORCH WAITIN for everybody to come out. I knew Ms. Rosie wanted to hurry so she could see why Poppa had to leave us and be at the church early. When Fanny was finished getting the girls ready, we headed up the road. We had about three miles to walk to the church so we stopped along the way to let the little ones rest and get out the sun for a minute. While we was resting, Harry Wood, the town drunk, was walkin up the road.

"Hey Ms. Rosie, how's y'all doin today?" He slurred.

"We's fine, Harry," she said.

"What y'all doin out here on the side of the road?"

"We's just taking a break from the sun. We is on our way to church."

"Oh, is Mr. Ernest comin back for y'all after he drop Emma and her chilren off? They just passed me bout thirty minutes or so, say they headed to church too."

Ms. Rosie ain't say nuthin', she just grabbed the girls' arms and start walking real fast up the road. I picked up Amos cause I knew he wasn't gone be able to keep up as

fast as she was walkin. She was on fire!

When we reached the church, we went and sat right next to Poppa. Ms. Rosie ain't say two words the whole service. Emma kept trying to get her attention but Ms. Rosie looked straight ahead. She probably wants to give her one of them phony waves that she always do. After service was over, Ms. Rosie got up and went and whispered something in one of the deacon's ears and then he went and whispered something to Reverend Waller. After that, they all came over to talk to Poppa. They took him in the back room and they stayed back there for about an hour. When he came out, Ms. Rosie, me, Amos, and the girls was sittin up in the buggy waiting to go home. I don't know what they said to Poppa in that room but it was the last day Emma ever rode in Poppa's buggy. That's how things was handled in the country. If you had trouble in your marriage, you went before the pastor and the deacons, and they'd straighten things out!

Things seemed to be goin okay and Ms. Rosie kept having children. Over the next ten years, she had Cathy, Ernestine, Walter, and Carrie. Right between the birth of Cathy and Ernestine, death came to visit my family again and took my baby brother Amos. He was scrawny and always sick. When Momma died, he was two years old and just never seemed to grow right. Ms. Rosie took real good care of him and tried to fatten him up and make sure that he ate, but he was still tiny for his age.

When he was eight, he came down with pneumonia

and never got better. After two weeks of being sick, he died. My sistas took it hard cause Amos was like they chile. They raised him from a baby, so they cried for days. Ms. Rosie was real hurt too. I always thought Amos was her favorite cause she kept him close to her hip and made sure us kids was lookin out for him. Ms. Rosie did all the plannin for his funeral. She made a real nice service and a lot of peoples came. Ms. Rosie sang a pretty solo that made everybody cry, it wasn't a dry eye in the church. After the funeral, Amos was laid to rest right next to Momma.

Ms. Rosie had three girls in a row and now that Amos was gone, Poppa was growin tired of Ms. Rosie having all these split tails. Even though they was the most beautiful babies in Hustle, Poppa wanted a boy to help out wit the farm work. When Ms. Rosie got pregnant again, we was all so excited for a boy after Clara, Cicely, and Cathy. We knowed that God was gonna give us a boy. We was gonna name him after Poppa and call him Ernest Jr.

It was so many of us chilren in the house and things was tight. My sistas from my Momma was big now and they was doin work for white folks, like washing clothes or runnin errands so they could make a little money to help out. My sistas from Ms. Rosie was still young so they would run around the farm all day and play. Clara would have to watch the lil ones while Ms. Rosie did the chores around the house. Clara didn't mind at all watchin the lil ones, she was real motherly and would do they hair and

act like their momma.

One day, Ms.Rosie start hollerin like a wild hog and we all came runnin in from the farm. We knowed what that sound was so Poppa got in the buggy to go get Ms. Estelle. The girls was tending to Ms. Rosie til Ms. Estelle got there. Once she got there, they was in that house for hours. We ain't even think about goin near the door cause they'd skin us alive. When it was just about dark, Ms. Estelle came out on the porch holding another baby girl. I will never forget the look on Poppa's face.

Even though he didn't look like he had no interest in the baby, he took her and said, "We gonna give God praise for a healthy baby. Her name gonna be Ernestine and we gonna call her Jimmie to remind us of how much I wanted a boy."

I think Poppa was hurt to lose a chile and he really wanted another boy to try to fill Amos' spot.

Within a year, Ms. Rosie was expecting again. This time ain't nobody get their hopes up for a boy cause it seemed like we was just gone have a family full of split tails. But on May 4, 1932, Walter May Fortune was born. Poppa was so happy, he finally had a son with Rosie and this boy was the spitting image of Poppa—long, pointy head and all. Two years later, Ms. Rosie gave birth to another girl and named her Carrie. Of all my sistas, she was by far the prettiest and looked like a livin doll baby. I took a real likin to her and would hold her all the time.

By now, all of my sistas from my Momma was older

and had moved up to Philly to look for work. My Momma had family up there and they always wanted my sistas to move up there after Momma died but Poppa was against it. Now that Poppa had all these mouths to feed, he let them go. I was grown now too, so Poppa helped me build a little house down on the farm and that's where I stayed.

Clara was about eleven years old now and with all the little ones in the house, she was responsible for a lot of the chores and not able to go to school no more. She did all the cookin and cleanin and even had to help with the farm when help was tight. Ms. Rosie would get little jobs helpin out the white folks wit they chilren or washing they clothes cause the farm wasn't bringing in enough to keep the family. Clara didn't mind helping out cause she was scared to death of Poppa. Especially when he'd been out drinkin and would come home fussing and cussin. Every time Poppa would come home drunk, all the chilren knew to run and hide. Clara would hide under the table in the kitchen. Her small body would fit up under there just right but her little fingers would be hanging out. Poppa would walk right on them in those big ole field boots, not even knowin that he had stepped on her fingers, makin them bleed. Clara wouldn't so much as whimper to keep him from yellin in her direction. Poppa was mean as a red snake when he was drinkin. He would come in and get to whoopin on Ms. Rosie like she was a chile. He'd take off his strap and whoop her just like she was one of us and nobody better get in the way or they'd get whooped too.

One time, when I was about thirteen, he was whoopin on Ms. Rosie and I tried to pull him off her. He blacked my eye and grabbed me by the throat and told me, "Boy as long as I feed you, you don't ever get in the way of me raising my family! Your ass will be off this farm so fast you won't know what hit you!"

When he let me go, I was gasping for air and from that day on, I would leave out when he would beat on Ms. Rosie. I couldn't stand to hear it, burned me up on the inside.

All them years of drinkin and smokin tobacco was startin to catch up to Poppa. He was always coughin and holdin his side. Every time he would cough, he was bringing up blood. I was doin most of the work on the farm now cause he was so weak and frail. Ms. Rosie kept beggin him to go see Dr. Berger, but these hard head men would rather wrestle a bear before they see a doctor. So, Poppa kept up with his ugly ways. Even though he was drinkin, cussin, fussin, and still whoopin up on his wife every weekend, you could see in his face that whatever he had was getting the best of him.

In the summer of 1938, Poppa took his last breath. All that drinkin, cheatin, and carryin on finally caught up to him. He came in barely able to walk one night after hangin out wit Bo Mitchell and the rest of his no-good buddies. He went to sleep and never woke up. When Ms. Rosie got up the next morning and found him, she was hollering so loud that I heard her all the way cross

the field at my house. I rushed over there to see what happened and when I walked in the door, I saw Poppa slumped over in the chair. I knew he was dead. All the chilren was sittin around lookin at Ms. Rosie.

Poppa was so mean that it seemed as if none of the chilren was sad. He was never close to any of us and not really the type of man to show love. I guess he showed his love by workin hard and makin sure we ate and had somewhere to sleep. But wit him gone, we ain't know how hard it was gonna be. He ain't have no money saved and come to find out, he had taken a mortgage on the land to help ends meet. It was startin to get cold and winter was fast approachin and the kids ain't have no coats or shoes. Ms. Rosie was makin the girls' dresses and pants out of potato sackcloth. I ain't never seen Ms. Rosie so sad, not even when Poppa was actin a fool. They was eatin potatoes every night for suppa and if it wasn't for Luke Harper's store up the road, I reckon they woulda starved. Luke Harper was a nice white man and wasn't like all the other white folks in Hustle. He would help us black folk by givin us credit for food and stuff until we could find a way to pay it down. Most of the white folk in Hustle hated colored folk and they made sure we knowed it. Ain't none of them cared if a colored family starved to death cause that was just one less family they had to kill.

During this time in Hustle, there was a lot of colored folk gettin killed and lynched by the KKK. They was some mean folks. One time, they set a farmhouse

on fire wit the family inside cause they said the nigger that lived there had looked at the Police Chief's daughter. Truth was, the white gal had a thang for black mens and was always f**kin some black boy. It was getting so bad that the Police Chief had to make an example outta somebody. Two people died in that fire but it was like it never happened because no one said a word. Nobody spoke up for fear they'd be next. That was another thing about Hustle, even though you was a free nigga, you ain't have no more rights than the animals that was on your farm. When them rednecks wanted to mess with the colored folk, it wasn't nobody to stop them.

Now that Poppa was gone, Ms. Rosie was a single girl and there was a lot of suitors that came knockin. All they was lookin for though was a wet ass, and that included a lot of Poppa's so-called friends. They ain't want no parts in helpin raise her chilren. Ms. Rosie wasn't that kind of woman though. She was strong and had respect for herself. When they came by, she was nice as pie and would bring out the whiskey and get them drunk as a skunk. Then, when they would pass out she would go through their pockets and take whatever was in them. When they would wake up and realize they money was gone, they wouldn't ask no questions cause they all had wives and shouldna been there in the first place! She would chuckle and say, "Get on home now, cause you knows you in trouble wit the Mrs." They knowed they was wrong and would just go on without causing a

ruckus. Ms. Rosie would use the money to pay down the bill at Luke Harper's or put it towards the mortgage that Poppa took out on the farm.

Ms. Rosie was a smart woman. One day some white men came and offered her some money to buy the farm. By the time they was leaving, Ms. Rosie had made a deal for them to rent the land. They was paying her and she got something from their harvest too. The money that she got was just enough to pay the mortgage on the farm, so she still had to find odd jobs to feed and clothe all the chilren. Ms. Rosie was able to pay the mortgage and the white folk that was renting the land hired me to help them work the land for the harvest.

I was coming up on twenty-five years old and was ready to start my own family. I still lived on the farm so I could help out and keep an eye on the Fortune girls, they was now reachin teen years. A few months later, I married Margaret. She was pretty and nice like Ms. Rosie and couldn't wait to have chilren. We ain't waste no time either. Within the first month, we was expectin and hoping for a boy.

CHAPTER 4

Meet The Fortune Gals

THESE FORTUNE GIRLS, AS THEY WAS KNOWN AS IN Hustle, was gettin big and frisky. Clara was fifteen now and likin a boy from King and Queen County named Dorsey Johnson. I ain't knowed much about him but I did knowed that I ain't like him. He be taking her to the Juke Joint and I'm hearing that she drankin whiskey and acting too frisky. One day I was coming back to the farm from the post office and who I seen over in the bushes by the barn f**kin but Clara and Dorsey.

I jumped down off that horse and buggy so fast and start whoopin Dorsey ass wit my belt and ran him off.

I said to Clara, "Ain't you got no respect for youself? Out here f**kin in the dirt wit this no-good nappy head boy."

She said, "We's in love and gonna get married!"

"Well he should marry you first before he have you out here rolling in the dirt! Mens don't want to buy the cow if they can get the milk for free!"

As Clara was scrambling to put her clothes on, I told her, "If I catch him around here again before y'all

is married, I'mma do more than beat his ass wit my belt. You hear me gal?"

Clara nodded that she heard what I had said but in her mind, she was in love and nobody was gone get in the way, including me.

All the girls was reachin they teen years except for Carrie. They was all frisky as the day is long, sneaking up to the Juke Joint and messin wit them no-good boys. The Fortune girls was makin a name in Hustle, just not the kind of name men kinfolk was proud of.

Two weeks later, Ms. Rosie asked me to go to run some errands and I seen Clara and Cicely walking down the road with ruby red lipstick on they lips.

I asked, "Where is y'all girls fixin to go?"

They looked at me and Clara says, "Our daddy is gone and we ain't gots to listen to you! We is grown and looking for our husbands."

I said, "Y'all ain't but fourteen and fifteen years old. Who but the devil told y'all that you should be looking for a husband?"

Cicely answered, "Seem like too many mouths for Momma to keep feedin so we gots to do our part."

I replied, "If y'all frisky tails don't get on this buggy right now, I'mma pull one of those switches off the tree and whoop your black tails all the way up the road!"

They hurried and got in the buggy cause they knowed that I was a man of my word. They also knowed that Ms. Rosie would let me deal with them the same way

Poppa would have.

While we was ridin to the post office, I told them, "Y'all gals is moving too fast and all these boys is looking for is a roll in the hay and once they get that, you won't hear from them no more. Y'all should be in school learnin somethin so you can get out of Hustle and see the world. You know your older half-sistas is up in Philly doin right good for theyselves. If you work hard and keep up your schoolin, you could go up there and do the same thing."

Even though they was mad at me, somethin in me let me knowed they was listenin.

When we got to the post office, I handed them my handkerchief and said, "Wipe that mess off your face for someone think the circus came to town."

They was mad all over again and rolling they eyes at me. I knew they didn't like what I was sayin but I knew that's what Poppa would have wanted. I picked up Ms. Rosie's mail and we headed back up the road. Before we could reach home, we seen about twenty KKK mens in their white clothes heading toward us. They had got so bold lately that they aint even wait for night to fall no more. I pulled the buggy to the side, and luckily, they sped right past us heading up towards Jim Dandy's farm.

Jim Dandy was a gamblin man and he probably owed one of them white men some money and hadn't paid up. When Cicely saw that they was headin up Jim Dandy's way, she started yellin and carryin on sayin, "We gots to help him!"

Now I ain't never seen nobody get so excited and want to go against the Klan.

I said, "Chile, what's done got into you and why is you so concerned bout Jim Dandy's affairs?"

She said, between all the cryin and snottin, "That's my boyfriend. We's gonna have a baby and gets married!"

I said, "Gal is you crazy? Jim Dandy is a grown man and you ain't but fourteen! How is y'all gone be married?"

She said, "We is! We in love and he wanna marry me. He was gone ask Momma if it's alright. Now the Klan gone kill him before he get to meet his chile!" She was cryin even harder now.

"Chile what is you talking about? See his chile?"

"I's pregnant," she said.

When she said that, before I knew it, I was heading towards Jim Dandy's farm cause if the Klan ain't kill him, I sure nuff was!

When we reached Jim's, there was no sign of the Klan. Maybe they was heading somewhere else. When I saw him coming out the outhouse, I jumped down off the buggy and ran over to him and grabbed him by the collar.

I said, "You done got my sista pregnant. She ain't but fourteen years old. You is a grown man! What you planning to do about this?"

Jim said, "Man, Hamilton, I swear before God I ain't knowed she was only fourteen. She was up in the Juke Joint flirting wit me. I asked her how old she is and she said eighteen!" He said, "Look at her. Do she look

fourteen to you? When I found out how old she really is, it was too late. She told me she was having my baby. I want a woman, not a chile lying about her age to get out of her Momma house. I ain't ready to be no daddy to two children—her and her baby! She lied and I don't want no parts of no baby wit Cicely and I done told her that!"

I let Jim's collar go and yelled for Cicely to come over.

"Cicely you done lied to this man and told him you was eighteen?" She didn't answer, but the way she looked at the ground I knowed that she did.

I told her, "Get your tail back on that buggy!"

I looked at Jim and said, "I'm sorry that she lied to you but you still gonna have to face Ms. Rosie and come up wit a plan cause you fixin to be a daddy whether you like it or not!"

I walked back to the buggy thinking, *dammit if only Poppa was here none of this mess would be happening!* I got back up in the buggy and we was quiet the whole way to the farm. When we reached the house, I told the girls, "Don't say nuthin' about what just happened til I figure out what we gonna do."

They both nodded and went in the house. Meanwhile, I'm tryin to figure out how I'mma tell Ms. Rosie that Cicely is havin a chile and that the daddy don't want nuthin' to do with the chile! It's hard enough for Ms. Rosie to keep food on the table for her chilren let alone adding another mouth to feed. About a week later,

when we finally did tell Ms. Rosie, she was so hurt.

She said to Cicely, "I wants more for you. I wants your life to be different from mines. I don't want you stuck on no farm strugglin to make ends meet! I want you gals to get out of Hustle and make a real life for yaselves. Cicely, you ain't ready to be no Momma so we gonna have to figure somethin out. You ain't but a chile yaself and I wants you to stay that way!"

The next day, Ms. Rosie made me give her a ride to Jim Dandy's farm cause she had a few choice words for him. Once we reached his farm, Ms. Rosie jumped down off that buggy so fast, Jim was stuck in his tracks and looked like he'd seen a ghost.

Ms. Rosie pulled out her pocketknife and said, "You round here actin like you ain't know that Cicely ain't but fourteen years old. You knew she wasn't no eighteen but you getting all the pleasure and don't want nuthin' to do wit what come from it. You is a weak man and God is gonna see fit that you pay for what you did. If you come sniffin around my Cicely again, you gone leave this earth wit your man part in your hand. Do I makes myself clear?"

Jim answered, "Yes ma'am, I'm so sorry. I won't bring no trouble to you ever again Ms. Rosie. I swear before God!" Ms. Rosie looked him up and down and put her pocketknife back in her bosom.

"I knows you ain't!" She said before rolling her eyes and walking back to the buggy. I ain't say a peep until

we was halfway down the road and Ms. Rosie bust out laughing and said, "Did you see how scared that devil looked?" We both had a good laugh as we headed back to the farm.

Cicely had to be around seven months pregnant when this fancy horse and buggy came out to visit the farm. A nicely dressed colored woman and gentleman got off the buggy and headed to the house. I could see Ms. Rosie waitin at the door to let them in. They stayed for about an hour before they got back on the buggy and rode off.

Later that evening, I asked the gals, "Who was those fancy colored people that came out to the farm today? Is Ms. Rosie selling the land?"

The girls shook their heads and Clara said, "No, those is the folks that's gonna raise Cicely's baby." Cicely looked real sad, but deep down she knew she wasn't ready to be nobody's momma. From that time on, we never mentioned it again.

A few months later, Cicely was in labor and Ms. Estelle was coming to birth the baby. The same midwife that had birthed them was now birthin their chilren.

When Ms. Estelle arrived, she said, "We done been down this road before so y'all know what to do. Fetch me some cloths and get the water boiling. We's gone have ourselves a new baby!"

After what seemed like forever, Cicely was done hollering and out comes Ms. Estelle with the most

beautiful baby girl. She was a pretty beige color wit jetblack curly hair. She was the prettiest baby in all three counties put together.

Once Cicely was all cleaned up and able to hold the baby, she said, "Her name gone be Belinda!" They let the baby stay wit Cicely for a few weeks so she could breastfeed and get the baby healthy for that fancy couple that was gonna come for her. I ain't never seen Cicely so happy. She gave all her time to caring for that baby. I was a little worried on how it was gonna mess wit her once baby Belinda was gone but I have to say, I was shocked by the way Cicely handled herself when the day came.

That same fancy buggy with the fine dressed folks pulled up to the house on May 21st. Cicely had Belinda cleaned up real nice and Ms. Rosie had given her some money to buy the baby a cute outfit and some sweet smellin powder from Luke Harper's store. All of the chilren was outside playin and they all said goodbye to Belinda when it was time for her to go.

Cicely kissed her lips and said, "I'mma always be your momma and you gonna always be my baby." She handed the baby over to the lady and then went to play jump rope wit the other girls.

I had done some meddlin to find out about this fancy couple cause I dare not get in Ms. Rosie's affairs. They was from Prince George's County in Maryland. Up there was some real fancy colored folks and they had money. The man was some kind of doctor and his wife had trouble

giving him chilren. When Ms. Rosie sent word to her kinfolk up there that her fourteen-year-old daughter needed a nice family to take in her baby, they was ready and willing. I was happy to know that my little niece was going to a nice home, but I was sad for Cicely cause I knowed her heart musta been in pieces. They was nice folks and told Ms. Rosie that they would bring the baby down once a year cause they wanted Belinda to know her real Momma and family. I think that might have been the reason Ms. Rosie chose them. Ms. Rosie loved her chilren so I know it hurt her to have to let this couple raise Belinda, but she wanted a better life for all of them.

CHAPTER 5

These Chilren Is Having Chilren

IT SEEMED LIKE AFTER CICELY CAME UP PREGNANT ALL THE Fortune girls was getting pregnant. Cicely got pregnant again but now she was sixteen so she had no intentions of givin this baby away. She had a baby by some married man from King & Queen County that ain't want nuthin' to do wit the chile again, but she ain't care. She named him Benjamin, after the man. He was a handsome baby boy wit caramel colored skin, big blue eyes, and a head full of curly black hair. Cicely had to start helping Ms. Rosie work for the white folk washin they clothes, cause she had brought in another mouth to feed.

Clara was expecting her first chile wit Dorsey Johnson, she'd been runnin around wit him since she was fourteen years old. At least he wanted to be there for his chile. Dorsey had a reputation for being a lady's man and also one that would go upside a woman's head. I wasn't so happy when they told Ms. Rosie that they was gettin married. I knowed that was gonna be a problem down the road.

When the day came for Clara and Dorsey to gets

married, I asked Clara, "Girl, is you sure you wants to marry this man?"

She said, in a sassy voice, "Yes I am! You want my chile running around here wit no poppa?" Fixing her hair she said, "I is happy. Me and Dorsey is in love and gonna raise our family together."

Well, she had made up her mind and I had done my part to make sure this was what she wanted. She asked me to give her away and Lord knows I didn't want to, but wit Poppa being gone I was next of kin. Walter May was still a little ole boy.

All of the sistas was done up all pretty and had their hair done up too. Ms. Rosie ain't seem too happy but she acted right nice for the weddin. Clara and Dorsey had told anyone wit ears that they was getting married so a right number of people turned out for the weddin.

It turned out to be a nice little wedding except Dorsey had some of his drunk ass friends there and they was eying the girls. It made me mad when the older men went after these young girls. Ernestine wasn't but twelve and Cathy was fourteen and they was cute as can be, looked just like Ms. Rosie spit them out. Ernestine was quiet and stayed to herself most times, so I watched her close. She wasn't as frisky as them first three gals. Cathy was the worst of the litter. Ms. Rosie had a time wit her! She had a mind of her own since the day she came out Ms. Rosie's womb. She was cussin and smokin by the time she was nine and no matter how many whoopings you gave that chile, it ain't

change her. I never did get how a chile so pretty could be so bad and mean. I noticed Aubrey Holmes was sweet on Ernestine and Paulie Saunders kept looking Cathy's way. Cathy was so mean that he kept shyin away every time she would look in his direction. It sorta made me chuckle for a minute.

Their weddin was nice. Clara was about eight months pregnant so Ms. Rosie had her a pretty off-white dress made by Ms. Paulette. All the girls wore yellow dresses. Them dresses and shoes cost Ms. Rosie a pretty penny but she always wanted the best for her gals. I knowed that Ms. Rosie's knuckles was gone be bloody from all the clothes she was gone have to wash for the white folks to pay them dresses off. Ms. Rosie ain't care nuthin' about that, she just wanted Clara to have a nice day. She really loved Clara for all the help that she gave her wit raising the chilren when Poppa died. It really hurt her that Clara didn't get to go to school because she knew Clara was smart as a whip.

The wedding went on into the night. Everybody danced, ate, and drank until well past midnight. It was sad for Ms. Rosie when the party was over and Clara left on Dorsey Johnson's horse and buggy and took off to go live wit him and his people. She ain't cry out loud or nuthin' like that but I saw her eyes well up and a tear roll down her cheek. I know she was gonna be alright cause she had them other three frisky girls to tend to, but they was big enough to tend to themselves now.

CHAPTER 6

Clara Getting Her Ass Whipped

A GOOD TWO WEEKS HADN'T PASSED BEFORE CLARA showed up to the farm wit a big, fat black eye and busted lip talking about Dorsey was beatin her.

"I'll skin him alive 'fore I let any man whoop on my gals!" I ain't never seen Ms. Rosie so mad.

Clara told Ms. Rosie, "After one week went by, he was actin like a mad man, drinkin, cussin and fussin for no reason, reminded me of Poppa." Then she said, "When I ain't pay him no mind, that's when he start hitting on me!"

Ms. Rosie said, "Well you ain't going back over there. This my first grandchile and I ain't gone let him kill it! Go on in the house and fix yourself up. The swelling will go down soon."

When peoples had troubles in they marriage, they usually go see Reverend Waller. But since Dorsey ain't never seen the inside of a church, there wasn't no hope in getting help. Once you married, kinfolk usually stay out of the affairs too. But Ms. Rosie just couldn't let it go. It was eatin at her insides. She was feelin like all the

years she took that mess from Poppa and ain't do nothin, she wasn't gonna let no man do that to her girls. Ms. Rosie was well liked by them white folks and rumor had it that she told the white family she was workin for what had happened to Clara. They saw to it that Dorsey got a whoopin of his own.

All I know is I saw Dorsey over at the saw mill and it wasn't a pretty sight. Look like mules had took to him and kicked his face in. When he saw me, he looked right pitiful and gave me a halfway nod. I guess he wasn't sure if I was gonna finish where they left off. But truth be told, I felt right sorry for him for a minute. Then I thought, that's what you get when you put your hands on a woman.

Clara stayed at the farm and in a few weeks had a baby boy that she named Dorsey Jr. Ms. Rosie ain't let Dorsey see his son for the first month.

Ms. Rosie said, "That's what happens when he wanna beat on the baby's momma!"

Clara was softenin up though and missed Dorsey. So when Ms. Rosie said he could come to the farm to see his son, she came a runnin to my house.

"Hamilton! Hamilton! Momma said Dorsey can come to the farm to see Dorsey Jr. Can you give me a ride up the road to fetch him? I really want him to see his boy!"

She was outta breath cause she came runnin so fast. "Let me get the horse and buggy ready and I'll take you." She was happy as a pig in slop!

Once we reached Dorsey's house, he was surprised to see us. He looked a little nervous but I guess after that whoopin he took, he ain't know what to expect.

Clara jumped down off that buggy fast as lightnin and went running to him yelling, "Our boy was born! He one month old today and my momma say you can come to the farm to see him. Does you want to come?"

Dorsey hugged Clara and spun her around in the air. He seemed real happy and said, "You knows I wants to see him and his momma too!"

All the way back on the ride to the farm, Clara was fillin Dorsey in on all the things that happened in the past month. She told him that the boy was a little small for his age and that he ain't eat much but he was cute as a button and looked just like his poppa. Dorsey seemed excited. Clara and Dorsey spent the whole day together with Dorsey Jr., just lovin on they boy. I really thought it was a nice thing to see. I gave Dorsey a ride back up the road that evening. He would come back every weekend to see his son and wife. This went on for about three months until Ms. Rosie let Clara go back and live wit him.

Before she let Clara go, she had a long talk wit Dorsey and nobody know what she said, but Dorsey never went upside Clara's head again. A few months went by and Clara was having another chile. Dorsey, Jr. was about nine months ole and he was a puny little ole thing but cute as the dickens. When Clara was about six months pregnant, Dorsey, Jr. fell sick wit pneumonia. We rushed him to Dr.

Berger and he gave us some medicine but within a week, Dorsey, Jr. had gone home to be with the Lord.

Poor Clara, I ain't never seen her so sad. For weeks, she wouldn't eat. She'd just sit on the porch staring at the sky. I imagined she was talkin to God and askin why he let this happen. But we was raised to know better and that God ain't mean and ugly like that, this was the devil's work. She wouldn't even let Dorsey touch her. It was like she ain't love him no more. We was really worried bout her. Ms. Rosie did everything to make her eat, told her she was killing the baby inside her. That's when she started eatin again.

The next months were touch and go. Clara spent a lot of time at the farm. I believe being around her kinfolk helped her get by. She gave birth to a baby girl and named her Juanita. She was a pretty little girl and looked just like Dorsey Johnson's sistas and momma. Clara was smiling from ear-to-ear, but there was still a sadness that she just couldn't hide. Over the next few years, she and Dorsey had another chile and named him Eldrige.

Clara was getting along better now and she was also livin back on the farm. She said she ain't want nuthin' to do wit Dorsey Johnson, she ain't love him no more. Now Ms. Rosie had her chilren and her chilren's chilren living wit her. The only good thing is that Clara and Cicely was old enough to work and help out and Ernestine and Cathy would tend to the babies while they worked. Ms. Rosie got them both jobs wit white folks washin clothes.

They seemed as if they was doing fine. They wasn't runnin up a big tab at Luke Harper's and was even able to buy a few dresses that they ordered from Sears & Roebuck. They would wear them when they went to the juke joint looking for new mens.

Cathy and Ernestine was coming of the age when mens was looking at them and wanted to take them out on dates. I thought they was too young at fifteen and sixteen to be going on dates. That's just how it was in the south, the younger the girl the more control men had on them. The old mens also like that they was the first to get the young pu**y. The girls in Hustle was just babies theyselves and should have been worrying about schoolin instead of worryin about finding a man. But most times, they mommas was tryin to pawn them off on men cause they was tired of taking care of them.

Cathy and Ernestine was thick as thieves and ain't have no interest in school. Ernestine was shy and not as hot in the tail as Cathy. Word around town is that Paulic Saunders was messin around wit Cathy and his raggedy, drunk friend, Aubrey Holmes was Ernestine's boyfriend. Neither one of them was good as two nickels rubbed together, but when you's a youngin, all you care about is looks. And these two was good looking fellas and all the girls was runnin after them.

I had been hearing rumors that the girls was fast, sneakin up to the Juke Joint and running behind these boys. But with all the workin I was doin and Margaret

about to have our second chile any day, I was busy and couldn't quite keep up wit them frisky gals like I used to. Ernestine had got so grown that she aint want nobody calling her Jimmie no more, we all had to call her Ernestine or she wouldn't answer. One day, I seen them walkin up the road.

"Come here girls, let me talk to y'all," I said.

Cathy came walking over to the buggy all frisky and said, "I hope what you want to talk about got to do wit giving us a ride to the store." Ernestine followed behind her.

"Girl, I ain't riding y'all nowhere. If you can make your way to the Juke Joint wit y'all frisky selves, you sure can make your way to the store!"

Cathy rolled her eyes and stood wit her arms folded. Ernestine shyly stared at the ground.

I told them, "If I catch y'all in the Juke Joint or get word that you in there before y'all reach eighteen, I'mma come in there with my belt and whoop y'all black asses back up the road!"

Cathy said, "You ain't our Poppa. He died long time ago."

"I may not be your Poppa but I's the closests thing you got to one. Poppa probably rollin in his grave lookin at what y'all Fortune gals be doing. You heard what I said and you know Ms. Rosie gonna back me. Now get y'all frisky tails on up to the store and rememba what I said. I'mma skin you alive."

Cathy rolled her eyes and walked off. Ernestine looked up at me like she heard me and gave me a little wave bye. It was like I was seeing the same thing happen to these two girls that happened to the older ones. I had hope for them, maybe to move up north wit they half-sistas and make somethin of theyselves. I didn't want them being stuck here in Hustle raisin chilren and washin clothes for white folks for the rest of they lives. Most of the girls wit no schoolin seems like that's all they could do in the south.

CHAPTER 7

Aint Worth A Penny

TALKIN TO THEM WASN'T WORTH A PENNY WIT A HOLE IN it! Three months later, that damn Cathy was having a baby wit Paulie Saunders! Folk ain't know much about him cause he wasn't raised in these parts. Honestly, I was hurt. I wondered if they life would be this way if Poppa was livin. Why am I such a bad brother that these Fortune gals is making all these babies and raisin them on the farm wit no poppas in they lives? Thinking about that cut me to the white meat. Poor Ms. Rosie was gettin tired too. She had raised Poppa's chilren, her chilren, now she got a house full of granchilren. You could see it in her face. It used to be round and always wit a smile but now it looked a little worried and more wrinkled than before. But there wasn't no time to look back. This chile was coming here in a few months.

Paulie did the right thing and married Cathy and they moved to a little house over in Tappahannock. They ain't have no big weddin. Pastor Waller's son was taking over preachin at the church, so he did Ms. Rosie a favor and came to the farm to marry them. Wasn't no way

neither of them could get married at the church. For sure God woulda sent lightnin and the whole church and all the peoples in it woulda burnt up.

I had seen some pretty babies before, and I thought Carrie was pretty, but they baby was sent straight from heaven. She was the closest thing I could imagine an angel to look like since Momma went home to be wit the Lord. They called her Conchita and she had pretty cocoa skin, big brown eyes, and cute little button lips and nose. I guess she really was an angel cause after only three weeks of being on the Earth, she went home to be wit the Lord.

This was the second baby birthed by a Fortune girl that died. Was they cursed or something? Cathy and Paulie took it hard but that ain't let it stop them from having more chilren. One year later, they had another beautiful daughter and they named her Denise. She was just as beautiful as Conchita and looked a lot like her too. A few years later they had a son they named Lorenzo. That boy was red with reddish blonde hair and ain't look like no one on our side of the family. His nickname was Lolo.

Paulie and Cathy was raisin they family on they own and would come visit Ms. Rosie on Sunday afternoons and they'd bring the chilren over to play wit Clara's chilren and now Ernestine's son, Butchie Boy. Ernestine had a baby the year before by that drunk, Aubrey Holmes. He ain't have no intentions on marrying her, so she was raisin the boy on the farm.

Ms. Rosie's house was full as a tick. She had her chilren and now her chilren was bringin up they chilren in the house and it only had three rooms. The house was falling down cause no men was around and the women ain't know how to do no fixing. Wit all them mouths to feed, it wasn't no money to pay nobody to fix it up. They was still stuffing hay in potato sacks to make beds for all them chilren to sleep on. I could only imagine with all the pissin in the beds them chilren was doing, the bed bugs or chinches had to be eatin they asses alive.

Walter May and Carrie was the youngest and the worst of both bunches of Poppa's chilren. They was the only two that ain't had no respect for they momma and neither one of them went to school past the fifth grade. Walter May would holla and cry for his momma all day at school, til they said he couldn't come back. Carrie was the same way, always wanted to be up Ms. Rosie's butt. I remember Ms. Rosie use to tell her and Walter, "Yall go on outside and play. If I fart, I'll save it in a bag so y'all can smell it when you get back." We use to fall out laughing.

Carrie watched the chilren all day while the older ones went to work for the white folks. Carrie was so mean to the little ones and would always be fussin about why she had to watch them. Walter was the spitting image of Poppa and was more like him than just looks. He was fast becomin the town drunk. Comin to the farm drunk, cussin, fussin, and kickin in the windows cause he wanted Ms. Rosie to give him money to buy more whiskey. When

I'd hear him actin up, I use to go over to the house to tear fire to his ass. Ms. Rosie ain't never want nobody to say nuthin' to him, that's why he carried on the way he did.

She told me, "Go on home Hamilton, I got him. Don't even bother yaself with this here fool!"

Every weekend when he'd get drunk, he'd kick out the windows in the house. He did the same thing until there was no windows left to kick in so they had to board up the windows wit wood. Walter came home one night and musta forgot or was too drunk to rememba and kicked the wood pane and broke his foot. He was hollering for Ms. Rosie to come and carry him to the doctor. She ignored him and wouldn't let nobody else help him either. She wouldn't even go wit him to visit the doctor cause she had to work and wasn't missin no pay. Ms. Rosie was fed up wit that boy and said she ain't care if his foot fell off. Walter never had it checked out and instead wrapped it in rags. That ole foot ain't never work the same again. Now, he walkin around wit a limp but still drinkin hisself crazy.

CHAPTER 8

May Day Event

MAY HAD ROLLED AROUND AGAIN AND IT WAS TIME FOR Hustle's big May Day Town Picnic. Well, it was more like an entire weekend instead of just one day. All the peoples that had moved up north would come back home and the folks who still lived in Hustle and the surrounding counties would come out too. They saved up their money to buy new outfits. Peoples cooked all kinds of food. Everyone looked forward to May Day.

My sistas from my momma would come back every year for this event. They had moved to Philadelphia soon as they got big enough to look for work. They would catch the bus back to Hustle and when they came, they had some mighty fine clothes and jewelry. I gotta say, my first set of sistas was some right fine women too. I'm sure they had boyfriends in Philly that was helpin them make ends meet cause all the womens from Hustle believe, "It's a poor mouse that has one hole." That mean you have to have more than one man helpin you out if you ain't married.

We was all getting ready for the big weekend and

everybody was excited to see the folks that had moved to Richmond, Washington, D.C., Maryland, and Philly. They would bring stuff back that we ain't never heard of or tasted so it was like we was getting to see a little piece of the world right here in Hustle. When my sistas, Mally, Gladys, and Betty got to town, I was down at the main road to pick them up. It was always good to see them, big city girls speaking the right way and always lookin fancy. They said that Fanny couldn't come cause she had to work and couldn't get off.

The first stop was always at Luke Harper's store and then out to the farm. They loved Momma Rosie and would bring her gifts and pick up food for the house. They stayed at my house cause there was no room for them at Ms. Rosie's wit all them chilren. They ain't really want to stay no nights there, Ms. Rosie need a lot of fixing up to the house. Like most folk in Hustle, there was still no running water indoors and peoples still used outhouses. Ms. Rosie's outhouse wasn't even working so, they kept a slop bucket in one of the rooms that they did they business in. The girls was too lazy and triflin to walk out back to take a sh*t. But my sistas never forgot where they came from and would fall right back in place, even though they had runnin water and inside toilets in Philly. Hustle was still they home.

Clara and Cicely was so excited cause the older sistas had missed the last May Day event cause they was working. So when they seen them in they fancy clothes,

hair styles, and jewelry, they was real excited.

Clara asked them, "Is y'all rich? Y'all look so fancy, like big city gals."

That's when Betty said, "No girl. We work and of course we have boyfriends that help us out when things get tight! There is a lot of jobs up north for colored women like us and they ain't all washin white folk draws!" They all laughed.

Gladys said, "I work at a diner, Betty is a receptionist at a insurance company, and Mally and Fanny work at a bank. Fanny has a white boyfriend and she has her own place so he can come over and stay with her from time to time. To get a job, all you have to do is take a test. If you can read, do a little math, and speak a little like white folks, they hire and pay you decent. Me, Betty, and Mally live together in West Philadelphia.

I could tell that this kind of talk was stirrin up somethin in Clara and Cicely. This was the life they wanted and couldn't find in Hustle. Is this the life that Ms. Rosie was talkin about when she told Clara that she wanted more for her girls than being stuck in Hustle rearin children? All weekend, Clara asked the older girls questions about life in Philly and they didn't mind sharing either. They told her about all the men wit real jobs, the bars and lounges, the jobs that were there for colored women, and so much more. They spent all weekend sharing their stories with the girls and the girls shared their sad stories of the slim pickins in Hustle and

all three counties wit them. It warmed my heart because I knew that Poppa and Momma was smiling down. Even Ms. Rosie was smiling this weekend, I'm sure she felt the same way.

When Monday morning came and the older sistas was getting ready to leave, there was sadness in Clara that I hadn't seen since the death of her chile. The older sistas had been home for the May Day event before and left and no one seemed to be bothered but this time was different. It was like Clara wanted to hop on the buggy and jump in their suitcase. Everybody noticed it, even Ms. Rosie. Clara was cryin and actin mighty funny this time.

Before we pulled off for the main road, so the older girls could catch they bus back to Philly, Clara said in a soft voice, "Can I write y'all and come for a visit?"

They all said at the same time, "YES!"

Clara lit up like a Christmas tree. She went running, "Momma! Momma! My sistas say I can visit them in Philadelphia. Can I go for a week and you watch the chilren? I'll work real hard so I can buy my bus ticket and leave some money to feed the chilren while I'm gone. Please Momma? Please, please, please?" She was beggin Ms. Rosie wit her hands like she was prayin.

Ms. Rosie looked and saw how happy this made her and said, "Yes!"

Clara did cartwheels all cross the yard. I ain't never seen a woman, or man for that matter, that happy.

Over the next few months, the girls sent letters back

and forth til Clara had saved enough money to buy a bus ticket and leave money for food for her chilren while she was gone. She ordered two dresses from Sear & Roebuck cause she ain't want to go up north looking raggedy.

When the big day came, we was all happy for her. Cicely looked a little jealous but she tried to act happy for her. Ms. Rosie fried a few pieces of chicken and packed some homemade rolls and preserves for her to take on the road.

Clara packed everything in a big brown bag that we got from Luke Harper's store. She hugged and kissed the chilren, said so long to her sistas and brother, hopped up on my buggy, and we headed to the main road. It made me feel good inside to see her so happy. She had a rough upbringing, with havin to help raise all of Poppa's and Ms. Rosie's chilren and now she raisin two of her own. She needed a break.

While we was riding up the road, I turned and said to Clara, "You sure is lookin mighty fine lil sis, like one of them city slicker girls!"

I seent her face turn red and she smiled and said, "Thanks Hamiltion, I's happy!"

Then she looked at me and got real serious and said, "I wants to thank you for all that you did to make this day happen for me. You think I ain't notice all them extra dollars in my savings can? I know nobody else that thoughtful. I want you to know you a good brother and been one ever since I was a young girl. You filled Poppa's

shoes in a lot of ways. You always respected and took care of my momma and the farm the best you could.

You tried to tell us fast tail girls to slow down and stop chasin them no good boys. I want you to know Poppa would be proud. You is a good man Hamilton and I's gonna make you proud."

My eyes watered up wit tears and one rolled down my cheek. I guess I needed to hear that cause I always felt real bad about the way them girls' lives turned out cause they ain't have no real poppa in the house.

I wiped the tear so she wouldn't see me cryin and said, "Those is some mighty kind words Clara and it means a lot. I'm always gone be here for y'all. Now let's get on up this road so you don't miss that bus!" I cracked the whip on Mr. Ned and said, "Yah! Let's get moving! My sista here got a bus to catch!"

The buggy sped up and we rode the rest of the way in silence, both thinking about what was ahead. When we got to the big road, I stayed and waited until Clara got on the bus. I waited all the way until she took her seat. She was smilin from ear-to-ear and wavin at me through the window. Something in me told me it'd be awhile fore I'd see Clara again and deep down, I was glad. I watched as the Greyhound bus pulled off and whispered under my breath, "I knows you gonna make me and the whole family proud."

CHAPTER 9

I'm Really Going To Philly

I AIN'T NEVER FELT MORE FREE THAN WHEN I WALKED DOWN the aisle and took my seat on that Greyhound bus. As the bus drove off, all my cares rolled away wit it. I couldn't believe I was really gettin out of Hustle. I stayed up the whole way to Philly just lookin out the window imagining what Philly was gonna be like from all the stories Gladys and them had told me. I tried to eat the food Momma cooked but the butterflies in my stomach wouldn't let me get nuthin' down. There was some man on the bus that kept lookin my way and tryin to catch my eye but I was keepin all my thoughts on Philly and wasn't thinkin bout no man. I chuckled to myself and turned my back so he couldn't see my face.

It was gettin dark and we could see all the bright lights as we got closer to the city. There was so many tall buildings and bright lights, I ain't never seen nothing like this before. All kinda cars was drivin and blowing they horns. It seemed like everybody was in a hurry or late to somethin.

Before I knew it, the bus driver was sayin, "Now

arriving in Philadelphia! Philadelphia last stop!"

I was excited and scared at the same time. All the peoples on the bus started getting off and I just sat there.

The man that had been lookin at me asked me, "Is you meeting someone here?"

I grabbed my bag close and said, "Yes, yes I is!"

He smiled and said, "Well then, you needs to be getting off this here bus so you can meet them."

I tried to look like I knowed what I was doing. I waited a few more minutes and then I got up to get off. I was praying to myself that my sistas was out there waitin for me, cause I was scared to death.

As soon as I stepped foot off the bus, I heard my sistas yellin and wavin sayin, "Clara! Clara! We over here!"

I lit up when I seen them. I ran over and hugged them and just kept thankin them for lettin me come. When I turned around, the man from the bus was standing there, so we all turned around and looked at him.

"You left off the bus so fast that you forgot your brown bag," he said as he handed me the bag.

I was a little shy and grabbed it and said, "Thank you."

"I hope you have a fine time here in Philly," he said before he nodded his head and walked away.

We all watched him walk off and when he was a lil ways gone, we started laughin.

Betty said, "Clara ain't been in town five minutes and already she turning the heads of these Philly men!"

We all laughed again while we walked to the bus stop. While we was on the bus, they started tellin me all about how to catch the bus and what lines take you where. They said you can get anywhere you need to go cause the bus goes everywhere. It wasn't like in Hustle, they ain't have no buses that you could take to get to nowhere. Back up in them woods, you had to walk everywhere.

Everything in Philadelphia was so different than in Virginia. The houses was all connected together and they had toilets that you pushed a handle and all the sh*t floated down. They had an icebox in the house to keep the food cold. They had runnin water. It would just come out anytime you turned the knob at the sinks. They even had something called a shower wit a bathtub. You just stood under the water and it would run on you while you washed up. We ain't never had nuthin' like this in Hustle. When we washed, we just used the basin. The first time I used it, I stayed in that shower for over an hour. I could feel years of dirt washin off me. I used some sweet smellin soap that made my skin soft and there was powder that left you smellin nice and fresh.

There was so many lights on the street at night til it still seemed like daytime and the cars was drivin so fast and always honkin they horns. In Hustle, we had the Juke Joint. But here in Philly, there was a bar on every corner. I remember laying on the bed just staring up at the ceilin thinkin about how I want this type of life. Then it hit me, this the first time I ever done laid in a real bed. Just then,

Betty came in. She grabbed one of the pillows on the bed and hit me in the head. I grabbed one and hit her in the head and we had a pillow fight like we was kids. We just fell out laughing. She said, "Clara, I'm so excited you're here! Tomorrow we gonna get our hair done and then we gonna go up to Market Street and do some shopping. Then, we're hitting the lounge tomorrow night!"

"Lounge? What's a lounge?"

She said, "Well, it's like the Juke Joint but nicer and with much nicer men that have a little change in they pocket." She gave me a high five and we fell out laughing again.

I said, "Betty, I had no idea that the livin up here was so much better. I mean, I seen y'all in them fancy clothes and all, but the way y'alls house is and the nice stuff y'all gots! Y'all even has a telephone! I want this type of life for me and my chilren."

She said, "And you are gonna get it, but first thing you have to do is stop saying chilren. It's chil-dren… with a 'D'. Say it, chil-dren."

I said exactly what she said, "Chil-dren."

"That's good! We gonna work on your English because up here most folks don't talk that country talk. They sound more proper and that's how you get a good job." I smiled real big and afta a few seconds, Betty said, "Guess what?"

I said all excited, "WHAT?"

"I asked my boss if you can come to work with me a

few days next week, and he said yes!"

I jumped up and down on the bed and started singing, "I's goin to work! I's goin to work!"

This was turning out to be better than I could have ever imagined.

"Now let's get us some rest because we have a long day ahead of us."

I was so tired from the bus ride that I probably was sleep in two minutes.

The next mornin, I was up before everyone. I tickled myself cause I tried to turn on that shower and got my whole head soaked. Good thing we was going to get our hair did. When Betty and them got up, I was dressed and ready.

Mally said, "Damn Clara, you in the city still getting up with the roosters."

I said, "It's more like gettin up wit the butterflies that been in my stomach all night!"

They all laughed. While they was gettin dressed I fixed us some breakfast.

Once we was all ready to go, I was so excited that I was shakin. When we got outside, I couldn't walk straight for looking all around. I ran into folks and almost got hit by the trolley. I never thought a train can ride down the middle of the road. Philly was the best place ever! When we left the hairdresser, my hair never been so straight. It was sharp as a tack. I told them that I wanted to see downtown before we went to Market Street.

Everyone was so friendly, even the white folk was mighty friendly, nodding and saying hi and a few of the mens even seemed like they was lookin at me kinda frisky like. I wasn't use to havin white mens talkin to me. I ain't pay it no mind until one man asked me my name and if Betty and Mally and them worked for me. I looked at him like he had three heads and said, "No, these here is my sistas."

He looked and said, "No, really, it's no way that these colored girls can be your sister."

I looked at him like he was crazier and said, "We are sistas!" He looked at us strangely and walked off.

They said, "Girl, he thinks you're white!"

I ain't never been mistaken for a white woman. Then again, everybody in Hustle and the next three counties know me, so they wouldn't think so. As the day went on, we noticed how people was treatin me a little different than they were treating my sistas. When we were in the city in them fancy stores, they would be very friendly towards me. They would look at my sistas like they had no business in the store or like they worked for me. We laughed and tried not to pay it no attention.

Once we got up to Market Street, this was more of where the colored folks shopped. As we walked around there, we noticed a couple of stares coming from some of the colored ladies, but we thought it was because our hair looked so good. When we got to 59th Street, we ran into one of Mally's friends and he pulled her to the side and I

heard him ask her, "Who's the white woman you with?"

Mally said, "She ain't no white woman. Everybody all day thinks that she is white. She is my sister from Virginia."

He was shocked and introduced hisself to me.

"Hi, my name is James, and you are?"

I said shyly, "Clara."

He said, "It's nice to meet you Clara. I hope you're enjoying yourself in Philly."

"Yes, well I just got here."

"Well then, I hope to see you at the lounge tonight. Your sisters are supposed to be coming."

They all chimed in and said, "We are coming!"

He said, "So, I'll see you later. Make sure to save me a dance." He smiled and walked away.

Now this was the kind of Philly man that I imagined in my dreams—tall, dark, handsome, and smellin good! I couldn't wait to go to the lounge.

Gladys said, "Come on, we have to get Clara a dress cause we know she ordered one of them dresses from Sears & Roebuck." They all laughed.

I said, "What? Philly girls don't shop at Sears & Roebuck?"

They said, "No girl, there are too many great dress shops in South Philly. We are going to get you something nice to wear so Mr. James will remember his dance."

They took me shoppin in South Philly and they ain't never lied. All the dresses was beautiful. The one they

bought me fit just right, I couldn't wait to wear it. They got me some nice lipstick, blush, and eyeliner too. I felt like a new woman once I got dressed. I looked like one of those city slicker women, same as they did. I never felt so alive in all my life! I knowed then that I could never live in Hustle again.

When we got to the lounge, I ain't never seen so many fancy colored folk in all my dreams. Ladies was done up with they hairstyles and faces full of make up. They had on fancy dresses and shoes, and they all had pocketbooks! The band was loud and playing some tune that I ain't never heard at the Juke Joint and people was dancing, drinking and smokin cigarettes.

That bass just did somethin to my body. I started moving to the music and seemed like everybody was starin at me. We made our way over to the section where some of Betty's friends was meetin us. All the way over, peoples was lookin at me. The looks from the mens was pleasant, but most of the ones from the ladies wasn't so kind.

When we walked up, Betty's girlfriend stared at me as she said to Betty, "I thought you was bringing your sister."

Betty said, "Girl, this is my little sister. What's wrong with you?" Betty gave her a very strange look cause she was just staring at me. I reached out my hand, smiled, and said, "Hi, my name is Clara."

She shook my hand and said, "I'm sorry if I seemed

shocked but when you walked over here, I thought you was a white woman!"

I said, "I figured so. Seems like half of Philly today think I'm white! They don't know this press out get wet, I'm Blacker than all these folks up in here put together!"

All the ladies bust out laughin. After that, it seemed like they knowed that I was Black and they treated me quite nice the rest of the evening.

I couldn't say that about all the women in the lounge. All night they was giving me mean looks cause all the men was giving me nice looks. I saw Mally's friend James, that I met on Market Street. I tried not to act nervous, but its somethin about this man that I likes. I turned around real quick and tried to act like I ain't see him but I could smell his cologne coming a mile away. When he came up and touched me on my shoulder, I turned around like I was surprised and said, "Oh, hi James!" I was tryin to talk proper like Mally and them.

He said, "Hi Clara, you look prettier than I remember from earlier." I felt my face turn blood red when he said it.

"Thank you sir."

"Sir is what they call my daddy. I'm James."

When he said that, I felt all warm and something gushed in my panties so I had to excuse myself and go to the toilet to clean myself up. I know he probably thought I was crazy cause I left so fast and in a hurry.

The lounge was in full swing. The band was playing and some lady was singing a jazz song that had the crowd

going. The dance floor was packed with women thrusting they asses all over the mens and the mens giving it right back. I couldn't see Betty and Mally nowhere so I pushed my way to the lady toilets and when I got in there, there was two ugly ass, nappy headed heffas fixin they hair in the mirror. I had seen them looking at me all night so I just went on into the toilet to handle my business.

As I cleaned myself up, I heard one of them say, "Ain't it a shame when white women have to come down to the club lookin for Black d**k? They get them a little Black girlfriend or two that get them a pass into the Black world.

Then the other one said, "But if daddy knew she liked Black d**k, he'd cut her out the will and disown her ass!" Then they both started laughin.

I was pissed! Even though I may look white, I wasn't! And I wasn't afraid to fight. Wit all the sistas I had, fighting was normal sh*t.

When I finished handlin my business, I came out and said, "I guess cause you thought I was white, I wouldn't say nuthin' to your nappy headed, ugly, Black asses. I happen to be Black and from Hustle, Virginia! Where I'm from, we don't have a problem beatin the sh*t out of heffas if they get out of line. Them girls you see me wit is my sistas and if they knew what you was sayin about me, we'd tear this place up! So I'mma wash my hands and finish enjoyin the rest of my night cause I'm gettin a lot of mens' attention!" I rolled my eyes and switched out. They

was lookin so shocked and confused and ain't say nuthin!

When I left out, I went to look for Gladys and them to tell them what had happened in the bathroom and also about James. When I finally found them, they had a drink for me.

Mally said, "Girl, where you been? James was looking for you."

I said, "I seen him and got too excited, if you know what I mean." I was looking down at my pu**y. They all bust out laughin.

Betty handed me the drink and said, "Drink this and relax."

I downed it and about fifteen minutes later, I was feeling real good. I seen James and even though he was talkin to some mens, his eyes was talkin to me while I was dancing and movin to the beat.

When he was finished talking, he came over and said, "Clara, where did you run off too?"

By now, I was feelin good so I ain't so shy. I started dancin real close to him and told him, "You do somethin to my body, somethin that I ain't never felt before. I likes the way you look, the way you talk, and the way you smell."

He smiled and said, "Well, I'm glad cause I haven't stopped thinking about you all day either."

He grabbed me close and we started dancin and grindin.

"I want to know all about you Clara," he said.

I could not believe this was happenin. I danced and laughed all night long before he gave us a ride home in his own car.

I ain't never knowed nobody that owned a car. I felt like a rich, white woman sittin up in that Thunderbird. When we pulled up at the house, Gladys and them got out the car and said they good nights. They was a little tore down.

"I had a real nice time with you tonight and I hope I can see you again tomorrow," said James.

"That would be nice!"

He leaned in and kissed me on my lips. I felt that same gush in my panties but this time I just let it sit in my panties all nice and warm while I thought about what his man parts would feel like up inside me. Once we finished kissing, I said, "Goodnight," and floated into the house.

Once I got inside, it hit me, what am I doin? I have two children back in Hustle that I have to get back to. I can't be here in Philly pretending that I have some other life. Those words that Momma use to tell us was coming back to haunt me. She would always say, "I want a betta life for you gals." Now I know what she meant. I just wish I could forget about Hustle and stay here forever!

CHAPTER 10

I Ain't Going Back

MY MIND WAS GETTING STRONGER AND STRONGER THAT I was not goin back home to Hustle. Even though we was hangin out late Saturday night, that ain't have nuthin' to do wit getting our butts up for church on Sunday morning. My sistas was members of National Baptist Church in North Philly. They stayed in West Philly so it was a thirty-five-minute bus ride. I ain't understand why they ain't go to none of the fifty churches that we passed in they neighborhood on the way to National Baptist, but that was they church.

We was all quiet on the bus ride, tryin to get the last bit of sleep before we got to the church. The service was good, the preacher preached a good sermon about God creatin a way out of nuthin! The choir could sing too and they only took up one collection. This was the first church service I had ever been to that only had one collection. Everything in my mind was lining up for me to stay except I hadn't talked to Mally, Gladys, and Betty about what I was thinkin. I ain't say nuthin, I just kept prayin to God to guide me in the right way.

Later on that evening, James came and picked me up and we went to dinner at some fancy restaurant in South Philly. I ain't never been to a restaurant in my life so I was nervous I wasn't gonna know what to do.

In the car I blurted out, "I ain't as fancy as my sistas. I lives on a farm and ain't never been to no fancy restaurant in my life. In fact, this the first time I been out of Virginia. I's been married before and gots two kids. If you wants to take me back to the house, I understand!" I was ready for anything that was gonna happen.

He took my hand and said, "I already know. When you disappeared last night, I had a chance to talk to your sister Betty about you and she filled me in. And you know what?"

I looked over at him shyly and said, "What?"

He said, "I knew all those things and I still wanted to go to dinner with you."

I leaned over and kissed him on his cheek. When we got in the restaurant, he showed me how to use a fork and knife the right way and which fork you use for what part of the meal. I felt so right wit him. I had the best time of my life. We didn't stay out too late on account I was going to work with Betty in the morning and we had to leave at 6:00 a.m. to make it to her job by 8:00 a.m. When he dropped me off, we made plans to have dinner once I got off from work wit Betty. I loved the city life. Yeah, I was missin my children and I knew Lil Juanita was missin me but I was having so much fun and it was only the second

day here.

When the clock went off at 5:00 a.m., I jumped up, excited to get ready. Gladys gave me a nice dress to wear wit some pantyhose and a slip. This dress was better for work than the dresses I had. I was flyin high, going to a real job instead of dressing in old rags cause I'm goin to work to wash somebody else's draws. When we got on the bus, I was shocked by all the peoples that was on the bus so early in the mornin. There was all kind of people on the bus, some had on suits, some had on maid outfits, some had on nice dresses, and some was dressed like cleaning men. Not one of them had on rags like what people in Hustle wore when we go to work. They all had jobs and looked like they was doin okay for theyselves.

My mind was getting stronger and stronger! How can I go back to Hustle? I'll die! It's no way that I'm going back even if I have to live on the street. I got a better chance here to make a way for my children and me. My stomach was sick wit worry I was gonna miss my babies!

When we got to the place where Betty worked, she gave me a few rules. "No loud talking. Don't touch nothing. Try to talk like me, Mally, and Gladys. Start practicing today. Listen to the way that I say things, repeat them in your head, and then whisper it under your breath, so you can get your English together."

I said, "Okay, I can do that," in my most proper voice. We laughed and walked into the office.

As soon as we entered, a middle-aged, nice looking

white man wit salt and pepper hair said, "Good Morning Betty!"

Betty said, "Good Morning, Mr. Silverstein!"

Then he looked at me and said, "Hello Miss, and what brings you in today?"

Before I could answer, Betty said, "Mr. Silverstein, this is my sister Clara. Remember I asked if I could bring her in to work this week because she's in town visiting and I didn't want to leave her at home alone?"

He looked confused and said, "Oh, oh yes, I do remember now!" Still looking confused he asked again, "And you said this is your sister?"

Betty chuckled and said, "Yes sir, I know what you're thinking. Clara looks white so how can she be my sister? We have the same father and her mother raised us both, so she is my half sister, but she is Black."

He said, "No need to explain anymore. Welcome Clara!"

I said, "Thank you sir!"

He was smilin and said, "Make yourself comfortable!" He showed me to a desk and said, "You can sit here." Betty was lookin at him a little strange cause he was being a little too friendly. I sat at the desk and start imagining if I had a fancy job like this and didn't have to wash nobody's draws. I giggled and spun around in the chair.

Mr. Silverstein said, "I'm going to get out of your way now but Betty make sure you show Clara here all that you know. I see a bright future here for her." He smiled

and walked to his office.

I covered my mouth to keep from screamin. I looked at Betty and said, "You heard what he said?"

Confused, Betty put her hand on her hip and said, "I don't know what all that's about cause he's never acted so kind to any woman that ever came in the door." She laughed and said, "I'm glad it's my little sister. Now let me teach you some stuff."

That was the moment when I knew that I would never live in Hustle again. I went to work with Betty for the rest of the week, she taught me so much. She worked with me on my grammar and math skills. Everyday, she would teach me the right way to say words and I started listening more and changing the way I talked. When Thursday night came and it was time for me to start packing up to go back home, I didn't want to go back. Problem was, I ain't have nowhere to stay. So, that night I prayed, Lord, I know that I ain't been the best person that I coulda been. I know that I coulda gone to church more than I did. But God, if you make a way for me to stay in Philly, I'll live better and go to church every Sunday!

On Friday morning when we got to Betty's job, we walked in and on the desk that I had been sitting at all week had a nametag that read, Clara Fortune. Betty and me looked at each other and then Mr. Silverstein came in.

He asked, "So what do you think about the new name tag?"

For a second, we both were silent and then I said,

"Is you saying I got a job? I mean, are you saying I have a job?"

He and Betty bust out laughin and he said, "Yes! I'm going to pay you $25 a week."

I screamed, "$25 dollars a week!" Before I knew it, I was hugging him and jumping all around! I realized that I was huggin my new boss, so I turned him loose and quickly apologized.

"Oh Mr. Silverstein, I'm so sorry for hugging you like that. It's just that I prayed last night for God to make a way for me to stay in Philly and here you is, I mean are, making a way!"

"I see something in you. I see that you and your sisters want to make a better life for you and your family and that's the kind of people that I want to employ around here. So let's get to work."

"Yes sir, Mr. Silverstein."

Betty was so happy for me. She said, "Girl, what arc you gonna do? You just took a job in Philly. What you gonna do with your babies? What you gonna tell Momma Rosie?"

"I haven't thought about all that. I just know I can't go back there, I'll die!"

She said, "Well you know Mally will let you stay with us especially now that you have a job and can help out with the rent."

"You think so? Do you think Gladys will be okay too? That was one of the things that worried me, where I

was gonna stay until I got on my feet."

"Girl, you gonna stay right with us until we can all get on our feet. Gladys wont mind at all."

I was happy. I had never been this happy in all my life.

Betty said, "But what you need to do right now is to write a letter to Ms. Rosie letting her know that you have a job and that you're not coming back for a couple of months."

I knew I had to do it cause Momma would have been worried sick if I ain't show up and ain't send her no word on my whereabouts. So, I told Betty that I'd write the letter later on that night.

All day I kept thinking about this new life that I was about to walk into. I thought about James and being able to be with a real Philly man that had something going for himself. I have a job and can start to make a way for Momma and my children. I thanked God for answering my prayers, and I promised that I'd be going to church this Sunday and every Sunday after that.

Dear Momma

Dear Momma,

 I hope you and the children are doing fine! Here's $10.00 to buy some food. I really like Philly and it's a good place for colored women to make somethin of theyself. I have a job making $25 a week. I'm staying with Mally, Gladys, and Betty in they place. They have a real nice place with a inside toilet, running water, a icebox, a stove, and a real telephone! Philly is so nice and the people here are real nice, too. Momma, I'm not coming back to Hustle right now. You always said that you want a better life for me, so I'm gonna stay here and make something of myself. Please take care of Eldridge and Juanita for me until I can come for them and I will send you money every week. Momma, please tell them that I love them and that I'm doing this for us, for all of us. I can help the family out more if I'm working in Philly over washing white folk draws for a dollar a day and wearing old rags cleaning toilets. I hope you're not mad at me and I'll be back as soon as I can. Please write me back and I'll send you more money next week. Kiss Juanita and Eldridge and tell my sistas I miss them. I love y'all! I'm gonna make you proud!

I promise.

Your daughter,
Clara

I took that letter to the post office and felt like my new life was just beginning! I felt bad cause I knew Momma and everybody was expecting me to come home today, but I had plans with James and for a moment, that made me forget all about being sad.

CHAPTER 12

Clara Didn't Come Home

WHEN THE GREYHOUND BUS STOPPED AND ONLY ONE man got off, I knew Clara wasn't coming back. What is I'm gone tell Ms. Rosie? This girl ain't came back? I waited about thirty minutes before I headed back to the farm. I knew Ms. Rosie was gonna be worried sick about Clara when I came back from the big road witout her. When I got back and went in the house, the look on my face gave it away that something was wrong.

After a couple minutes, Ms. Rosie said, "Hamilton, where is Clara?"

I told her that she wasn't on the bus. She stopped cookin and came over to where I was standing and said, "I sure hope nuthin ain't happen to that gal. She was supposed to be on that seven o'clock bus!"

She was startin to look real worried now, pacin back and forth and sayin under her breath that she knew she shouldn'ta let Clara go. Then she started prayin, Lord, please don't let nuthin happen to that gal, these here chilren need they Momma! Then the tears started rollin!

"Ms. Rosie, don't get yaself all worked up. You knows

that these girls is fickle!"

I hated to see Ms. Rosie cry since I was a little boy and Poppa was whoppin on her. I always left and that's the same feeling I had now. I told her that Mally and them has a phone so I'm gonna get the number from my house and go on up to Luke Harper's to see how much he'll charge me to make a call to Philly!"

Luke Harper was one of the few people in town that had a phone and he was the only one that let the colored folk use it for emergencies. Ms. Rosie seemed a little at ease when I told her that. I went back to the house and started lookin through all the old letters that Mally and them had sent me with they phone number til I finally came arosss it. I made my way on up to the store cause I knew Ms. Rosie was sick wit worry. When I reached there, Luke wasn't there but his wife Ms. Ellie was. She said Mr. Harper wouldn't be back til the mornin. She must have seen how down I got when she said that cause she asked me what was wrong.

I said, "My sista Clara ain't come back on the bus from Philly today and Ms. Rosie was worried sick. I wanted to know how much Mr. Harper would charge me to make a call to my sistas up in Philly."

She said, "Oh Lord! Rosie must be just about crazy wit worry. I tell you what, I'll have Luke go on and add it to your bill. You come on here and use the phone and find out what's goin on with your sista Clara!"

I was so thankful! All I kept saying is, "Thank you

Ms. Ellie! May the Lord bless you and your family!"

She let me come around the counter and I handed Ms. Ellie the letter wit the phone number and she start ringing they phone. I had so many butterflies while it was ringing, first ring, nobody answered, second ring, then the third ring. My heart was beatin so fast I thought it was gonna jump out my chest. Then, on the fourth ring, no answer. Finally, after the fifth ring, I heard, "Hello?"

"Hey there girl, this Hamilton. Who this I's talkin to?"

"This is Gladys, Hamilton! It sure is good to hear your voice!"

"Yours too! But look here Gladys, Ms. Rosie worried sick Clara ain't showed up on the bus today. Did she get on the bus?"

It was quiet for a few seconds and then Gladys sighed and said them words that I already knowed in my heart. "Hamilton, she's not coming back right now. She has a job making $25 a week and she wants to make a life for her and her children up here."

She told me that Clara wasn't home, but she wrote Ms. Rosie a letter telling her everything. She said to tell Momma Rosie not to worry, that they are watching out for Clara and to give her a few months and she'll be back."

I was quiet for a minute cause I knew that news was gonna hit Ms. Rosie right hard. She really depended on Clara and now she had her two youngins to raise.

"Gladys, I'll let Ms. Rosie know but you let Clara

know that she done broke her momma's heart!"

"Hamilton, I promise that Clara is gonna make the family proud. In one week, this girl is making a name in Philly and it's a good name, so y'all don't worry. She'll be back home to visit in a couple of months."

We said our goodbyes and I hung up the phone. I thanked Ms. Ellie once again and told her that Clara was just fine. She was stayin in Philly a little longer and that Ms. Rosie would have some money real soon to pay down the bill.

When I left out that store, and all the way back up to the farm, I thought about how I knowed that girl wasn't gonna come back down here to Hustle once she seen Philly. I just asked the Lord to bless her, my sistas and me too once I told Ms. Rosie that she wasn't coming back.

When I told Ms. Rosie what Gladys had told me, she said, "Hamilton, what in the devil is you talkin about that gal staying in Philly? Who gonna look after her two chilren? How is I'm suppose to work and feed and care for them witout they Momma?"

Ms. Rosie was yellin and slamming stuff all around the house.

"Clara done lost her cotton pickin mind just say she ain't comin back and think nuthin here about these chilren and how they gonna fend witout they momma! They daddy ain't worth the stink off sh*t, and now they momma done ran off to Philly! Lord, give me strength!"

She went and sat in the rocking chair and I seen the

tears rollin down her face. She said when she see Clara, she gone kill her, bring her back to life and then kill her again.

I left her alone cause I knew she was hurtin. When I went outside, I saw Juanita sittin underneath the tree by herself. I guess she was missin her momma and wondering where she was. Eldrige, Benjamin, and Butchie Boy was runnin around playin and throwin stones at the chickens. Them boys was always gettin in some kinds of trouble. I felt right bad for what was comin for Ms. Rosie.

I guess Ms. Rosie had told Cicely and Ernestine about Clara stayin in Philly cause they came over to the farm askin me all kind of questions.

"Hamilton, did you talk to Clara? How she gone leave her chilren here wit us while she up in Philly? When is she comin back?"

I cut them off before they could go on ranting and raving and said, "Wait a minute! Like I told Ms. Rosie, I ain't talk to Clara. I talked to Gladys and she said Clara ain't coming back, that she workin and she gonna come back in a couple months to visit. I don't know no more than I told Ms. Rosie. Gladys say Clara got a good job, and that she gonna make us proud and make somethin of herself."

Cicely was mad as can be and she was the one askin all the questions.

She said, "Well, we all wants to make somthin of ourselves but we ain't run off and leave our chilren wit our

momma first chance we get. Clara is a selfish hussy! And when she come back I'm gonna let her know!"

She left out and headed on down the path. Ernestine was still standin there with her hand on her hip and pattin her foot and said, "Hamilton, can you really go to Philly and get a job and make somthin of yaself?"

I answered her and said, "Seems that way. Your older sistas and now Clara ain't came back." I seen the same look in her that I did Clara. Once she able to get away, she gonna be gone too. Her only problem was runnin around wit Aubrey Holmes.

By the end of the week, Ms. Rosie got the letter from Clara with $10 dollars in it. The letter said what Gladys had told me. So, since Ms. Rosie already knowed, she was happy to get that money to pay Luke Harper and get some more food. The bill for all the food they had got on credit was about four dollars and then Luke charged her account one dollar for the phone call to Philly. She had money left over to get food and things that the chilren needed. Ms. Rosie was startin to think that Clara being in Philly might not be so bad if she was able to send money home like this.

Things was okay for a couple of months. Clara was sendin money every week so they was all able to eat and pay the little bill they had. She never made mention of when she was comin home in her letters but the money she sent helped out. Ms. Rosie, Cicely, and Ernestine went to work for the white folks and Carrie watched the

kids while Walter slept all day before he went out at night and drank hisself to death. Things seemed to be getting along right good and we was all settling into life wit Clara bein gone.

CHAPTER 13

Surprise Baby

ONE SATURDAY, ME, MARGARET AND OUR BABY, JOHNNY Mae, was getting ready to go to King & Queen County to visit her momma. Carrie come runnin down the path yelling, "Hamilton, Momma say come quick somethin wrong wit Jimmie, she hollerin that she gots bad pains in her belly!"

Everybody except Carrie had stopped calling Ernestine by her nickname cause she liked to get under Ernestine's skin. My Poppa gave her that name back when she was born cause he wanted a boy. I always thought she was too pretty to have an old ugly boy's name, so I always called her Ernestine.

"Pains in her belly? Did she eat somethin bad?"

Carrie said, "I don't know what she ate but the way she hollerin seem like it's eatin her!" I told Margaret to keep gettin ready and that I be right back.

When I got cross the farm, I heard her just a wailin. That wasn't a sound of somebody that ate somethin bad! When I got in the house, Ernestine was sweatin, and breathin hard and screamin for bloody mercy.

I said, "Girl, what in the dickens is wrong with you?"

She yelled, "I don't know, but please run get Dr. Berger!"

So, when she asked me to run and get Dr. Berger, I thought back to when this girl fell out the big oak tree in the yard and had a big gash on her leg and she ain't want no parts of the doctor. Now I'm thinkin this ain't no jokin matter if she askin to fetch the doctor.

I went back cross the farm to tell Margaret what was goin on and get the buggy. She said she was gonna go over and help out while I went and fetched Dr. Berger. When I gots to his house there wasn't nobody there. I start thinkin to myself, todays is Saturday! What am I gonna do? I'm thinkin the way this girl is hollerin, I gots to get some kind of help. The closest person I knowed to a doctor is Ms Estelle. So, I rode on down to Ms. Estelle's place and thank God she was home. On Saturdays, a lot of peoples went visiting and handlin they business around and about like me and Margaret was fixing to do.

I jumped down from the buggy and Ms. Estelle came on the porch and said, "Hey Hamilton, what bring you around here?"

I say, "Somethin wrong wit Ernestine and Dr. Berger ain't around and she hollering like crazy that somethin wrong wit her belly!"

Ms. Estelle asked me if she ate something bad.

"I don't think so wit the way she hollerin!"

She said, "Wait, let me run and get my bag!"

When we got back to the farm, all we heard was Ernestine hollerin. When we walked into the house, we seen Ernestine down on a cot on the floor. Ms. Rosie and Cicely was over top of her and a baby's head was stickin out of her and blood was everywhere. I turned around and walked back outside cause I seen that this girl was in labor! I never seen no chile bein born. I was feelin light headed, so I sat on the porch.

I heard Ms. Estelle say, "Oh Lord, this gal is far along! Y'all gone have to hurry and get the water boiling and get some more rags!"

Cicely said, "Once we knowed what was going on we started the water and Margaret went to run and get some mo rags!" Then here come Margaret runnin across the field wit a hand full of rags.

Ms. Estelle asked everyone except Ms. Rosie and Cicely to go on and wait outside. Everybody was in shock cause no one even knowed that Ernestine was pregnant. She wasn't but sixteen and Butchie Boy wasn't quite two and here this girl is wit another chile. She needs another chile like she need a hole in her head, specially wit that drunk Aubrey Holmes, if that even who the poppa is! Wasn't about but thirty minutes or so before Cicely came out holding the new baby. She said this here is Ernestine new baby girl, her name is gonna be Lil Cicely. Ernestine named her after me, say she remind her of me. All I could think was Lord, another mouth for Ms. Rosie to feed!

I just couldn't believe this girl done carried a chile for

nine months and none of us knowed! I seen this girl dang near everyday and ain't knowed or had a clue that she was having no baby! Ernestine was a big boned tuff old girl, wit strong legs like a mule. She was quiet and stayed to herself most of the time, but let anybody mess wit her sistas or brothas and she was the one that would fight the gals or dem crazy country boys just like Fanny.

About two weeks went by for I seen her or Lil Cicely, her new baby. She stayed in the house cause I guess she was right shamed of what she did. Hiding that she about to have another chile and ain't got a half decent poppa for neitha of them.

So, first thing I said when I seen her is, "Girl what is you doing around here havin another chile? You barely can feed Butchie Boy, and they poppa ain't sh*t but a low down drunk. What is you thinkin chile? You askin me can you go on up to Philly to make a good life for yaself and all you doin is makin it harder for yaself!"

She was lookin down at the ground and lookin right pitiful and she answered me and said, "When I asked you about goin to Philly to make a betta life for myself, I knowed then that I was pregnant. I was thinkin about what I was gonna do. I know Aubrey ain't worth his weight in water so I'mma have to make a betta life for me and my chilren."

I looked up cause I heard someone fussing coming toward us, it was Carrie. She came over and said, "Hamilton, you thinks it fair that Clara, Cicely, and

Jimmie keep havin chilren and her Momma want me to stay home all day and watch them?"

Before I could speak, she yelled, "I AIN'T GOT NO CHILREN AND I DON'T WANT TO RAISE NOBOBODY ELSE'S! Momma think cause I don't go to school that I got to helps out while they go to work. She don't make Walter May drunk, lazy ass help out!"

In a way, I heard what she was sayin but she ain't wants to do nuthin but lay around the house all day and Momma was taking care of her too, so I knew what Ms. Rosie meant.

I tried to tell her that's what family does to make the ends meet, everybody got to help out. I told her about when my Momma died and how I had to take care of Fanny, Mally, and Gladys and them and how Betty was a little bitty baby. But she ain't want to hear nuthin I had to say cause I ain't side wit her so she walked off and threw her hands in the air and said, "One day, I'mma leave this farm and see how y'all fair wit all y'all bastard chilren!"

Now one thing was true, Aubrey's momma, Ms. Laura, was a good woman. She was a God-fearing woman that'd raised Aubrey by herself. They say his daddy was a drunk too from over in Tappahanock, but no one ever seen him. Ms. Laura worked for this white family cookin and cleaning for about twenty years and they was real good to her. Ms. Laura had a lil house on about one acre of land and a lil bit of money, that's how Aubrey was able to stay drunk all the time. When she heard that Ernestine

had another one of Aubrey's children, she came out to the farm to see Ms. Rosie. A lot of women wouldn't even come around thinkin somebody may want somthin from them. But she wasn't like that, she was gonna make Aubrey take care if his chilren. She told Ms. Rosie that she know it's hard on her raising all these chilren and they poppas ain't nowhere to be found, but she ain't gone put Aubrey's mess on her. She said that Ernestine could move to her farm and that it had plenty of room for them chilren to grow up right nice.

Ms. Rosie was growin tired cause she told Ernestine that she was gonna have to live with Ms. Laura and Aubrey and try to make a family for theyselves. And wit all the lip that Carrie is giving her about watching another chile, she felt like God had sent her an answer. Ernestine was not happy but she knew that it was the best for her Momma, and the chilren. Ms. Laura would be able to help her wit the lil ones and they would have a roof over they heads and food in they bellies.

Ernestine had been stayin on the farm with Ms. Laura and Aubrey about four months and she and Cathy would come visit Ms. Rosie on Sundays and bring the kids. Cathy and Paulie is still living over in Tappahanock and was doing good for theyselves. But Aubrey was actin more like a fool than he was before. He was drinkin more and more and starting to stay out all night. Word was that he was makin and sellin moonshine, everybody around here know that's the white man's business and no colored

folk should go near it wit a ten foot pole. Ernestine say that Ms. Laura nice and all but treat her like one of the chilren, don't really let her be a momma to her kids, Butchie Boy and Lil Cicely even calls her Ernestine.

People was startin to talk more and more about Aubrey makin and sellin this moonshine. See one thing about Hustle is that people loves to talk about other folks' business, it's just the way it was in a small town. They say Aubrey was workin wit Lionel Johnson, a colored man from Carat County. This town got a lot of Black folks that can pass for white. So, Lionel Johnson looked white and I think sometime he really thought he was. They say that during slavery, the slave owners from Carat County only slept with the slave women. They ain't want no part of they wives and so after awhile they wasn't makin no white chilren. It was a lot of mixed chilren and they had chilren together so the whole town got a lot of them geetchie lookin folks. Peoples say they a little funny that they marry cousins and brothers and sisters just to keep the white look in the family blood.

One day, Ernestine came to Ms. Rosie's farm. She said that Aubrey hadn't been home in three days and her and Ms. Laura was worried. She said the last time she seen him was when him and Lionel Johnson left the house a few days ago and he ain't been back since. She told her what Aubrey and Lionel was into and that colored folk can't mess around wit white folks' money. She said that her and Ms. Laura told him to stop being around Lionel,

that he wasn't no good. He ain't want to listen, actin like a big shot wit all these big plans on how he gonna make money. She told him that Aubrey better wise up and Lionel wasn't nuthin but trouble.

About three more weeks went by and ain't nobody knowed or heard nuthin about Aubrey. Ms. Laura went to the police but they ain't care about no missin nigger, specially the town drunk, so they ain't put no effort into findin him. Another two weeks had passed when Ms. Laura, Ernestine, and the chilren came out to the farm. Ms. Rosie sent Walter May to come and get me, say they found Aubrey. When I reached the house, Ms. Laura was weepin. She said, "They found my boy in the woods over behind the saw mill stabbed and beat to death! They say they could barely know it was him, but he had his pocket watch that I gave him some years ago."

Ernestine was cryin and looked scared to death and said, "Momma I'm scared to stay at that farm. I'm scared for me and the chilren!"

Ms. Rosie said, "Gal, you can always come back to this here farm!" She told Ms. Laura that she was so sorry for what happened to Aubrey. She asked her if she wanted to stay at the farm for a couple days til things blew over. Ms Laura said, "I ain't gone let nobody run me from my farm that I worked my blood, sweat, and tears to buy! I'mma stay right there!"

I gave Ms. Laura a ride back out to her farm. She had a lot of plannin to do to get ready for Aubrey's funeral.

CHAPTER 14

James Is My Man

I WOULD WRITE MOMMA EVERY WEEK AND SEND HER $10 BUT almost two years had passed by since I left Hustle. Ernestine had a new baby girl, Aubrey was dead, and I hadn't been back for none of that. Now it was coming up on Christmas. Things were going great for me in Philly. I was learning how to speak right and type at my job and I was even doing some of the paperwork. Most of the time, I was just greeting the clients and making sure they were comfortable while they waited. Mr. Silverstein had taken a real nice liking to me. I think sometimes Betty was jealous, cause he gave me a lot of attention.

I didn't care nothing about him though. I was in love with James. Me and him was going real strong, matter fact I hadn't seen or been with another man since the second day I got to Philly. I still paid my rent and everything to Mally, and most of my things were there, but I stayed most my nights with James. He wasn't like no man I knew from Hustle or any county in Virginia. He knew how to treat a woman and make me feel like a woman. We had a good thing between us!

James knew that I was worried with how long it had been since I'd seen my momma and children. He knew that even though I was enjoying my new life, a part of me was sad cause they weren't in Philly with me. One night, after he picked me up from work, he told me he had a surprise for me. When I asked him what it was, he said, "What's the best Christmas present I could give you?"

I thought about it and I didn't even know what to think of because nobody ever asked me what I wanted for Christmas. The couple of Christmases before he gave me a pair of pearl earrings and a bracelet. But I didn't ask for anything and wasn't really used to getting gifts. The most we'd get as kids was some fruit and nuts in an old shoebox. I shrugged my shoulders and looked blank and said, "I don't know."

He said, "How about we drive down to Virginia to see your momma and your children?"

Before I knew it, I had jumped up and was hugging his neck so tight he couldn't breathe. He was playing like he really couldn't breath, and I just kept hugging, kissing, and thanking him! I couldn't help but to thank God for sending me such a wonderful man. I couldn't believe that somebody was this nice to me. That night, James and I made love in ways I didn't even know were possible. In all my years, I had never felt so safe with a man. I could open up to him about things I had never told no one else. No man I knew ever had as much wisdom as James and he was handsome and had some money. I was a blessed girl!

When I told Gladys and Betty that I was going home for Christmas, they wanted to come too.

"Shooooot! We're not passing up a free ride to see the family," said Gladys.

The only thing left to do for me and Betty was get up the nerve to ask Mr. Silverstein for the time off. We wanted to visit for a long weekend. Christmas was on a Sunday so the plan was to leave a halfday on Friday and be back in the office on Tuesday. We had it all worked out. I was going to ask him for the both of us cause we knew he was sweet on me.

On Monday morning, I went to his office and asked if I could speak with him after lunch. He asked if everything was okay. I said, "Yes." He told me to come back to his office at 1:00 p.m. When I came back to my desk, Betty looked at me and showed me that her fingers were crossed and I showed her that mine were too.

The morning was busy as usual and after lunch things slowed down. It seemed like time was flying today just because I had to ask Mr. Silverstein if we could have some time off. I mean, it shouldn't be a problem. We work Monday through Friday from 8:30 a.m. to 6:00 p.m. and sometimes on Saturday from 9:00 a.m. to 2:00 p.m. if business was good. When 1:00 p.m. came around, I couldn't get up out of my chair fast enough and Mr. Silverstein was coming out of his office to remind me of our meeting. We walked back into his office and I was about to sit down when he said, "Close the door behind

you."

I walked back and closed the door, then sat in the chair across from his desk. He had a slight smile on his face but also a look of concern.

"What is it Clara? Is everything alright? Do you need anything?"

"No sir, I'm fine. It's just that, well, it's been a couple of years since I've seen my children and my momma. So, me and Betty was wondering if we could leave early on the Friday before Christmas and have off on the Monday after Christmas so we could go home and visit our family?"

He let out a breath of air like he was relieved from some pressure and said, "Is that it?"

"Well yes, what did you think I wanted to talk to you about?"

"I thought you were going to say that you found another job or that you weren't happy!" He went on to say, "That will not be a problem. You can even have off that Tuesday as well. You should really spend some time with your children! I'm even going to give you a $25 Christmas bonus so you can buy everyone nice Christmas gifts!"

I was starting to believe I was in a dream. How were things going so good for me?

"My family is gonna be so happy. It's been years since we've all been together for Christmas!"

That's when he said, "But Clara, Betty has to stay. Someone has to be here to open the office on Monday.

Betty is aware that my family and I go to visit my wife's family in Florida and I come back on Tuesday. Betty will have to open the office. You haven't seen your children in almost two years, you have to go!"

"But sir, this year is different. My friend is taking us down so it wouldn't cost us anything so we-" he cut me off in the middle of my sentence.

"Clara, you have small children and you did end up staying for two years when you were only suppose to visit. So, I understand you needing to go home. But Betty needs to be be here on Monday to open the office. I'm sorry."

He said again, "Clara, I'm sorry," and I knew I couldn't get him to change his mind.

"Yes sir, I understand."

I was feeling right sick because I knew Betty was waiting at the door to hear what he said.

Before I walked out of his office, Mr. Silverstein said, "And I'm going to put that bonus in your next check so you can start your Christmas shopping!"

He smiled and I gave a little smile back and said, "Thank you, Mr. Silverstein. My family really appreciates your kind gesture." I have never in my life had $50 at one time.

When I went back to my desk, all kind of things ran through my mind. Should I lie and just say we have to be back on Sunday? Do I tell her that he's giving me a Christmas bonus? I wasn't sure if he was giving her one.

Betty stared at me then asked, "So, what did he say?"

One thing I knew is that my Poppa would roll in his grave if he thought some white man came between his girls, so I told Betty what he said.

Betty tried to act like she wasn't mad but I could tell, you could have fried an egg on her forehead. She was slamming papers for the rest of the day and she didn't say two words to Mr. Silverstein all day and usually they were chummy. He must have known that I had told her cause he stayed clear of her too. Betty didn't have much to say to me either. I could tell she was really pissed off over the bonus cause I kept hearing her say, "I worked here for three years and I never got a $25 Christmas bonus! She come here in less than two years she getting a $25 bonus and she started at what took me two years to get to!" I didn't say anything because I knew she had every right to be mad at Mr. Silverstein.

All the way home on the bus Betty didn't talk much. I tried to act like I was looking out the window and then I just looked at her and said, "So, we gonna let this come between us? Betty, I can't help the way this man treats me. I have never had anybody treat me so nice, but I don't want this to come between us."

She turned to me and said, "This isn't just about the way that Mr. Silverstein treats you it's the way everybody treats you. Ever since you been here, things just been lining up for you. Everybody's been eating out of the palm of your hand cause you look white! When I came

here, it wasn't that easy. I had to work for everything I got, and it's not fair! I deserve a bonus, but what do I get?" In her Mr. Silverstein voice she said, "Oh, let Clara take the front desk so she can greet the clients as they come in!" She went on, "I've been sitting in that desk for a whole year before you came! It just isn't fair Clara!" She turned back and looked straight ahead so I just left it alone.

Betty was acting real funny, barely speaking to me at home or at work. Gladys told me not to worry about it but me and Betty was real close and I didn't know why she was mad at me. Then, one day out of nowhere, when we was on our way to work she said, "I don't care what Mr. Silverstein say, I'm going home for Christmas!"

I looked at her and said, "You sure? Who's gonna open the office on the Monday after?"

"I don't know and I don't care!"

Ever since she made up her mind that she was going anyway, things between us went back to normal. Neither one of us mentioned to Mr. Silverstein that Betty was going home to Virginia for Christmas.

CHAPTER 15

Clara Is Coming Home To Visit

DECEMBER 23RD HAD FINALLY ARRIVED! I WAS SO EXCITED I couldn't sleep the night before. I packed all of my clothes and all the gifts I had bought for the children, Momma, Hamilton, and everybody else. I bought Juanita the prettiest dresses, skirt and blouses, with new shoes and bows for her hair. She was going be the prettiest, sharpest thing in Hustle. I bought all my sisters' children clothes, shoes, and coats too. With that bonus and the money I'd been saving, Christmas was going to be real nice this year!

When noon hit, me and Betty was grabbing our coats and purses. We wished Mr. Silverstein a Happy Hanukkah and left out. James had already picked up Gladys and all of the bags so he was outside the office waiting for us. We jumped in the car and off we went to Virginia! We laughed and talked all the way to Maryland then Betty and Gladys fell asleep. Mally couldn't come cause her boss wasn't giving her off on the Monday after Christmas either. And Fanny never came around since she had this white boyfriend. It seemed like in order for her to be with him she couldn't have nothing to do with

her family.

While Betty and Gladys was asleep I said to James, "You know I really appreciate you taking me home to see my family. I want you to know that we live humble. I told you that our family is real poor. Where we come from is nothing like Philly, so I don't want you to think less of me cause of where I come from."

"Clara, I don't know how many times I have to tell you, I love you cause of you. Not where you come from, not cause of what you have. I like you cause you are a hustler. Where you come from means something real special. You are from Hustle and it's in your blood. There's more than one way to hustle." He winked and gave me a smile.

I thought about what he'd said. Nobody ever made me think about being from Hustle in a good way. I didn't even know what it meant to hustle, but I knew by the way he said it, it meant something good.

I had drifted off to sleep when James said, "Y'all sleepy headed girls wake up! I think we're here!" I rubbed my eyes and looked around. We were home! I sat up and told him, "Turn right here!" We were on the big road. As much as I hated Hustle when I lived there, it felt real nice to be back. Lord knows, I didn't have any plans of staying even if I had to walk back to Philly with the kids on my back! I thought in my mind how that might look and I chuckled to myself. Betty and Gladys told James all the places as we passed them by and James was just looking.

He didn't seem shocked the way I thought a city slicker like him would look at a place like Hustle.

In my last letter to momma, I didn't tell her that I was coming home cause I wanted to surprise her and everybody. As we were getting closer and closer to the farm, I got more butterflies. Once we got to the farm road and started heading down, it was pitch black and you could barely see in front of you. All of the dust was kickin up and I knew James' shiny car was dirty as an old mule. I had never been in a car coming down these old roads so I was a little scared. When we were getting close to the house, I saw a light come on inside. I'm sure Momma could hear the car coming up the road.

When we got there, we all jumped out the car and was heading to the door. Suddenly, it swung open and Momma stepped out holding a shotgun. "Who is dat?"

Benjamin, Eldridge, and lil Butchie Boy was standing on the porch too. Benjamin was holding a rifle and he was only eight years old. They taught all of us how to shoot at a young age.

I froze and said, "Momma! It's us, Clara, Gladys, and Betty!" I saw her put the rifle down and she started coming close and said, "Clara, Gladys, and Betty?"

"YES!" I went and hugged her so tight and just kept kissing her all over her face! By then Gladys and Betty was hugging her too.

Betty said, "Momma Rosie, you was about to blow us away!" James was just standing back watching and

smiling.

Momma said, "Gal, why you ain't tells me in your letter that you was coming home? I would have tried to fix up a lil bit or fix myself up a lil more."

"Momma you are fine!"

She said, "Who that man and who car is that? And y'all drove in that car all the way from Philly?"

I said, "Momma this is James, my boyfriend." He came and reached out his hand for Momma's hand and kissed it and said, "It is very nice to meet you ma'am. You have raised some mighty fine girls."

Before Momma could say a word, Benjamin, Eldridge and Butchie Boy were outside lookin at the car. Benjamin said, "Greeeeat day! I ain't never in my life seen nuthin like this. Man, this is a nice car!"

Him and the boys was walking all around the car. They had got so big since the last time I seen them.

"Eldridge, you'd rather look at a old car than come hug your Momma?" He walked ova and hugged me around my waist. It wasn't the way I had pictured it in my mind, but I guess he had to warm up.

That's when Betty said, "Y'all big headed boys get over here and give your aunties some love!"

When I turned back round, Carrie and Juanita was standing in the doorway and there was a beautiful lil brown skin girl with jetblack curly hair, I knew that was lil Cicely.

I said, "Jaunita, it's your Momma! Come here girl

and give me a hug!"

She walked to me real slow and hugged me and then walked back and stood next to Carrie.

That's when Carrie said, "Ummm Huhhh! That's what happen when you leave your chilren for almost two years. They don't know you no more!" She rolled her eyes and walked back in the house.

Momma said, "Clara don't listen to that gal. She mean and hateful!"

By now Hamilton was at the house with his rifle cause he heard the car coming up the road too. He was so happy to see us.

"Y'all girls was about to get hurt driving on out here in a car late at night! I'm surprised the police ain't stopped y'all. Colored folks driving in this fancy car! Y'all sure is a sight for sore eyes!" He hugged us all.

"Hamilton, this is my boyfriend James Smith and that fancy car belongs to him!" Hamilton grabbed his hand and grabbed him in and hugged him tight.

"You must be a right fine man to drive my sistas all the way back home from Philly!"

James was smiling and barely breathing from the tight bear hug Hamilton had him in. He managed to say, "It's nice meeting you too Hamilton."

He came over to me and whispered, "You and your family sure do give some tight hugs." I elbowed him in his side and smiled at him.

We all went in the house and sat around talking. I

saw that Juanita and Carrie were acting a little different towards me, but I figured I'd just give them some time. I asked Momma where Cicely and Ernestine were and she said in a sassy way, "Where they is every Friday night, up at the Juke Joint hoeing around!"

James looked at me, surprised that my Momma would say something like that but he didn't know ole Rosie!

I said, "What do you mean Momma?"

"You heard what I said and I'm tellin you right now ain't no more chilren coming in dis here house! I mean it, I ain't raisin not a nare notha chile!"

That's when Carrie said, "Well you the one lets everybody bring they chilren in here and leave them for you to raise. It's your own fault!"

Now James is lookin real nervous and I seen where this was headed, so I just said, "No one is having more children!"

Carrie said, "Listen at her, now she talkin all proper like she white!" And rolled her eyes at me.

Hamilton must have seen things was getting ugly cause he quickly changed the topic and said, "Ms. Laura told me that they may knowed who killed Aurbrey."

Betty asked him, "Who did they think did it?"

Hamilton said, "I think they just be telling Ms. Laura any old thang cause she walk up to talk to the sheriff once a week to see what they found out. I felt right sorry for her cause she right pitiful and on the farm all alone. She

go to work everyday, to see the Sherif on Thursday, and to church on Sunday. She don't never have no visitors and Ernestine don't never take the kids to see her. Only time she see them is for a quick minute if Ms. Rosie take the chilren to church."

"That's a shame. Ms. Laura is a nice lady. I hate that things turned out for her the way they did," said Gladys.

Betty said, "Even though Aubrey was about to drink hisself to death, he still didn't deserve to die the way he did."

Momma said, "They ain't bit more lookin for Aubrey's killer than I am! Them white folks tell you anything you want to hear!"

Just then, Cicely and Ernestine came busting in the door. Cicely was yelling, "Momma whose car is that in the yard?" When she saw us, she looked surprised.

Ernestine said, "Hey yall!"

She was really happy to see us. She came around and gave everybody hugs. Cicely spoke to Gladys and Betty and gave them hugs and then she walked over to James and said, "Who this nice lookin city slicker?"

I went over and stood right next to him and said, "Cicely, this is *my* boyfriend, James Smith."

He held out his hand and said, "Very nice to meet you Cicely. I've heard a lot about you."

Cicely ain't shake his hand and said, "Ohhhh, well we ain't heard nuthin bout you. Is you the reason that Clara ain't come back home in two years when she got to

Philly and left her kids here for Momma and us to raise?"
James was looking like a deer in headlights! I know he
didn't think he was going have to put up with this type
of mess.

I said, "Cicely that has nothing to do with him. If
you have somthing you want to say to me, just say it!"

Cicely said, "You got some nerve! You send Momma
a letter sayin you wasn't comin back home. You ain't care
nuthin about how Momma was gonna make it or how
your chilren was gonna make it! All you cared about is
Clara and how Clara's gonna make it!"

I said, "That's not true Cicely! I helped raise all y'all
and Momma will tell it! For one time, I thought about
me. I knew I could be more help to Momma and all of
y'all working up in Philly!"

That's when Carrie said, "You think you can send
money and that's gonna replace these here chilren
Momma? They don't care nuthin about no money when
they up cryin at night or they sick!"

I told them both that I didn't care about what they
thought. My plan was to get my Momma and children up
and off this farm.

Cicely said, "You is a selfish heffa!" and slapped me
across the face! Enough was enough. We went at it! We
were punching, slapping, and scratching at each other's
faces. James finally broke it up and pulled me outside.

"Clara, I didn't come here for this! Now if this is
what it's gonna be like this weekend, we can get right

back on the road!"

I was crying and so ashamed! All I kept thinking is how ungrateful my sisters are. It didn't take $10 a week to take care of two children in the south so some of that money was making sure they ate too!

Momma came out on the porch and said, "I hope y'all gots all your bad blood out cause if you cut up again, I'mma tear the skin off both y'all asses! Y'all two go on stay with Hamilton. Gladys and Betty gonna stay here. We got the outhouse fixed so they be just fine."

I hugged Momma and told her I'd see her in the morning.

"Now tomorrow, I don't want no foolishness out of you and Cicely or none of y'all simple actin gals, you hear me?"

"Yes, ma'am!"

Ernestine came on the porch and asked me if I was all right. I told her I was fine and she said, "I's glad you home and we all did miss you!"

I smiled and said, "See y'all in the morning."

CHAPTER 16

I Ain't Missin Nothin

THE NEXT DAY WHEN WE WOKE UP, I WAS SORE AND STIFF as can be. I still had Cicely's hand print across the right side of my face. James and I weren't used to sleeping together in a small bed and all that fighting with Cicely didn't help. I could smell the country bacon, eggs, home fries, grits, and biscuits cooking. That Margaret sure did know how to cook! That musta been how she got Hamilton's greedy self. I had already told James that he would be washing in a basin so he was ready. Once we got ourselves together, we went and had breakfast with Margaret and Hamilton. We talked for awhile but I wanted to hurry and go to the house to spend time with Eldridge and Juanita. When we got to the house, they were just finishing up breakfast too. Since I had been sending money, everybody sure was eating a lot better.

I asked the children, "Are y'all excited that Santa Claus is coming in a day?"

Benjamin said, "He don't never bring us what we want!"

I said, "Well this year, I heard something different.

I heard he has a lot of presents for y'all cause you've been good and you helped take care of Momma!"

He lit up and said, "You think he might bring me a baseball so me and Elleeboo can play catch?"

I said, "I think he might!"

Elleeboo is a nickname that we gave my son Eldridge and we gave Benjamin the nickname Benji. I looked at my sisters and said, "He may even have a few things for some ole funny acting wenches!" And I rolled my eyes. I went over to Juanita and said, "I know he has lots of pretty dresses and doll babies for you!" She looked up at me and smiled and hugged my neck.

I said, "So we have to get ready! Christmas in the morning! We have to go to the store so we can get some food to cook for Christmas dinner. This is going be the best Christmas the Fortune Family ever had."

Walter May came downstairs looking hung over. When he saw us all sitting there he said, "Look who back from the dead. So you decide to come back and be a momma to your chilren?"

Before I could answer, Momma said, "Boy shut your simple ass up! It ain't no worse than me still takin care of your simple ass and you a grown man!"

We all laughed and didn't pay him no mind. Cicely and Carrie didn't want to come to Tappahanock with us, so they stayed at home with Momma and the kids. When we drove in town to the store, so many folks was staring at us. Not too many folks in Hustle ever seen a car. We

stopped at Luke Harper's store first and when we walked in, Ms. Ellie looked and said, "Clara Bell is that you?"

"Yes, Ms. Ellie, how are you?"

"Well I'm just fine. You had your momma worried sick when you didn't show up on the bus two years ago!"

"I know, but I got a job and all…"

She looked James up and down and said, "That ain't all you got!"

I looked at James and he was red as a cherry. I told Ms. Ellie that James was my boyfriend and she said, "I see why you ain't come back around these parts!" Then she gave me the thumbs up. I laughed and told her that Philly was a nice place and I was doing real good there. When I finished my shopping, she said Philly must be good with all the food I was buying and how Momma and them wasn't running a tab no more.

In a town small like Hustle, word traveled fast so somebody must have told Dorsey that I was in town. He and Alvin Taylor came up to Luke Harper's. When I saw him coming, I told James who he was in case he was up to some funny business.

He walked up to me and said, "Girl, you do know we is still married and you gonna just up and leave for Philly and leave these chilren here wit your Momma?"

"Dorsey Johnson, you better get out my face. You know we wasn't together before I left and that we wasn't gonna never get back together so don't come up here acting all crazy."

"Girl, don't raise yo voice at me!"

"Dorsey, go about your business. When the last time you checked in on the children? You sure haven't taken them something to eat. So don't try to act like a poppa and husband now!"

Dorsey looked like he was ashamed. I know he wanted to hit me so bad but he didn't know who James was and Dorsey was no fighting man.

"Now you talkin and dressin all fancy cause you done left and went up to Philly but I want you to know one thing, you's a sorry excuse for a Momma! You can leave a man behind, but don't no real Momma leaves they chilren behind!" He tipped his hat and him and Alvin walked off.

I grabbed James' hand and started walking to the car. I was so tired of fussing with folks and from the look on James' face, he was too. It was a good thing I had told James the truth cause this mess would make any man want to run the other way. I tried not to let Dorsey's crazy self get to me, but I started thinking about how I just left my children with my Momma. I always kept coming back to the truth that it was the best decision for us all. I knew I was missing out on a lot with my children, but in my heart, I hoped it all worked out in the end.

When we got back from Tappahanock, Momma told me that she made Walter go in the woods and chop down a tree. Betty had bought a box of Christmas balls with us so we could make the tree look nice. We took in

all the bags and everything seemed to be okay. Cicely and me weren't talking much but we weren't being mean to each other either. Momma said that Cathy, Paulie, and the chilren was coming over after church for Christmas dinner. It sure was going be good to see Cathy cause she was funny and cussed like a sailor. It was also good that her and Paulie were doing well. Cathy would have whooped his tail if he stepped out of line.

We cooked and talked late into the night. The children were excited cause for the first time, they expected to get things they wanted on Christmas morning. I was more excited than the children because I had gotten them so many presents, I couldn't wait for morning. Once everybody was sleep, James and me started bringing in all the gifts from the car. I had packed two big old suitcases, one with all the new clothes and one with all the new toys. The house was smelling good, a mix between all the food and the pine tree. Once we set everybody's presents up, we fell asleep in the chairs.

The children came running downstairs in the morning, I don't even think the roosters had crowed. When they came down and saw all the toys they went crazy! They were yelling and saying they knew there is as Santa Claus. Little did they know that I was Santa. I was just so happy to see them so happy. Juanita and Eldridge seemed real happy too. Juanita was playing with her new baby doll and Eldridge played with his new truck. Benji got his baseball, lil Cicely had a baby doll too and they

had jump ropes, jax, cards, toy guns, and even a sling shot. They all had brand new outfits too!

Momma and the girls finally came down from hearing all the noise the kids were making. When they saw all the toys, their eyes got big as fiftycent pieces! They said "Girl, you done robbed a toy store?"

"No, I saved my money!" I handed them all their presents. They all opened the boxes and start screaming. I got all four of my sisters new dresses from a boutique on South Street. They were fancy dresses that cost me a pretty penny. I had four boxes for Momma. The first two she opened was a church dress and coat. The third was a church hat to match and the last was a pair of shoes. The shoes had a little heel to them and this was the first time that I knew Momma to have a shoe with a heel. She put the shoes on and got up and started dancing all around!

"Gal, they gonna think I'm the First Lady when I shows up this mornin in this here outfit!" We all laughed. It felt good to see my family so happy.

Christmas was not cheap but Mr. Silverstein had told me about joining a Christmas Club. I took $5 dollars out my check a week and in December the bank gave it back to me so I could use the money for Christmas shopping. He said that way, I would always have money at Christmas time to buy presents. It worked out good for me cause I started in August and by the time December came around, I had saved $100.

After church, Cathy and her family came over to the

house. Cathy still never went to church. She was the rebel in the family and said anything that came to her mind.

When she came in the house the first thing she said was, "Who is this good lookin man here, cause I knows he ain't from around here?"

"Cathy this is my boyfriend James."

"If the mens look this nice, maybe I should run on up to Philly!"

I gave her a hug and then she said, "Hey there girl, you lookin right good. Philly and James must be treating you right!" She was giving me the eye like he handles his man business.

"Girl, you still crazy!"

Denise and Lolo had gotten so big. Denise was a precious, brownish red girl with long black silky hair like Momma. She looked like a little doll baby and was real sweet and polite. Lolo was a cute, red, mean lil ole thing with red hair. We always said he must look like Paulie's people. Paulie looked good too, he looked a little weary like he needed some rest. Momma said that he worked three jobs to take care of his family cause Cathy wouldn't work.

We sat around and ate and talked all night. Paulie and Cathy didn't leave until about nine o'clock. As they were leaving, I told Betty that she better run and catch a ride with Cathy and them, maybe they would take her back to Philly in time to open up in the morning for Mr. Silverstein. She looked at me and rolled her eyes.

"I'm not thinking about Mr. Silverstein!" She went on about her business talking and eating.

I stayed up late playing with Juanita and Eldridge cause I knew we were leavin at noon the next day. We played until about midnight when they fell asleep.

Once I laid them down, Cicely came in the room. She hadn't had much to say to me since the fight. When James saw her, he got up and said, "I'll let you two have some time to talk."

When he left she said, "I's sorry for what I said and for slapping you."

"Umm huh."

"Clara, I was jealous, okay. You need to hear me say it? I want to leave Hustle too. I was mad that your chance came first."

I looked over at her and saw the tears filling her eyes. I went and hugged her and told her I was sorry too and that I hadn't planned on staying in Philly but things just started working out so good for me.

"I knew it in my heart, but it still ain't stop me from wishin it was me!"

"It's no reason that you can't come too. Just this time, we have to do it the right way. No running off and nobody knowing what the plan is!"

We smiled and hugged each other. The rest of the night I sat up telling her all about Philly. We talked, laughed, and giggled. Momma had to tell us to quiet down before we woke up the children. Cicely swore

before God that she was coming to Philly before the year
was out.

CHAPTER 17

Can't Wait To Get Back To Philly

ELDRIDGE, JUANITA, AND MOMMA CRIED THE WHOLE TIME as we packed up the car and got ready to leave. Of course, I was crying too. I promised to visit every three months and James promised that as long as he was around, he would bring me back. That seemed to put everybody's mind at ease. I felt bad about leaving but I couldn't wait to get out of Hustle. I was going to miss everybody but nothing could make me stay.

Once the car was loaded and we had kissed everybody, we headed towards the big road. A relief came over me that made me feel like I was really free. I had the blessing of my family to stay in Philly to work and make something of myself and I was going to do just that. My plan was to get them out of Hustle too, if it was the last thing I did. I thanked God because I knew he was real and he had answered my prayers.

Betty was in the back and she was quiet like the cat stole her tongue. She was probably worried sick cause she knew she was supposed to be at work opening the office.

I looked back at her and said, "Betty, you haven't

said two words since we got on the road. Are you getting homesick?"

"Nobody is homesick, more like work sick! I don't know what excuse I'm going to give to Mr. Silverstein about not opening the office today."

I knew she was thinking about that. James asked her with a puzzled look on his face, "You were suppose to go to work today? How did you plan to do that?"

Betty said, "I didn't plan to. I knew that we wouldn't be back but at the time, I was mad and didn't think I was being treated fairly! Clara could have off to go home for Christmas but I had to stay and open the office and I've worked there longer than her. But now I'm nervous!"

"Well what's done is done. But being honest is the best way to go," stated James. He told her that she should have talked to Mr.Silverstein before she didn't show up for work though. It was quiet for a minute and I guess Betty was thinking about what he said.

All of a sudden, Gladys bust out laughing and said, "Did y'all see Alvin Taylor? I can't believe I wanted to marry that fool!" We all bust out laughing.

Betty said, "Girl, you would have had all his funny looking babies with those big ole jug heads!"

I added, "With the droopy eye!" We all hollered. James just shook his head.

For the rest of the ride back, we talked about people in Hustle and our friends in Philly. We were trying to keep Betty's mind off of work and Mr. Silverstein. We

finally reached Philly about 4:00 p.m. and we dropped Betty and Gladys off at the house. We told Betty that we'd pick her up for work in the morning. James always gave us a ride when I stayed at his house.

As we drove to his house, I asked if we could go to Maggie's Soul Food Restaurant to grab a bite to eat. I wasn't in the mood to cook after being on the road all day. When we got there, the place was sort of empty so we sat at a table by the window. While we were walking to our seats, I noticed three women sitting at one of the tables. By the way they kept looking at us, something in my gut told me that they must've known James. The waitress came over and took our order and the women were still staring in our direction. Then they started talking loud and saying, "Men ain't no good!"

I was looking at James and he was looking at the menu and trying to act cool. I didn't know why he was still staring at the menu cause the waitress had already took our order.

"James, those women keep looking over here at us and now they're talking all loud saying how men ain't no good. Are they talking about you?"

Without looking up, he said, "I don't know those women."

Just then one of them said, "Look at him with his next victim. If she knew what I knew, she'd run away as fast as she could!"

They all laughed. I looked at them and they were

looking dead at me!

"James, you're gonna tell me that you don't know these women and they're looking right at us?"

"Clara, don't let those foolish women ruin our dinner. We had enough mess this weekend!"

"Ruin dinner? They're ruining our dinner by starting mess! And what are they talking about?"

James got up from the table and walked out leaving me sitting there looking like a fool! When the ladies saw him leave, they laughed even more. One of them said, "If you can't take the heat, get on out the kitchen!" That made them laugh even harder. When I realized that he was heading to the car, I grabbed my purse and ran out of the restaurant. I knew that my face was red cause I was embarrassed and mad!

When I got in the car I asked, "Why did you run off and leave me sitting there if you didn't know those ladies?"

"Clara, I ain't into getting into no argument with a woman! It's a lot of people that think they know me or want to know me and if you're going to be my lady then you have to get tough skin! Ask yourself, who do I sleep with every night? Who did I just take to Virginia to see her family? Don't ever question me about what no foolish woman say."

I couldn't say anything, he was right. We were together all the time and he treated me better than any man I ever knew. We didn't say a word until he pulled up

at the hoagie shop and asked me what I wanted to eat. I thought about how those women were eating their soul food and how I was about to eat a hoagie. I made up in my mind to never let what anyone says about my man change how I feel about him. He was a good catch and all those women were just jealous.

James didn't have much to say for the rest of the evening so when we went to bed, I showed him, in more than one way, that I was sorry for what happened earlier and that I appreciated him taking me down to Hustle.

The next morning, we were back to normal. He was up cooking breakfast while I was getting dressed for work. When we got to the house to pick up Betty, she looked pale and sickly. I wasn't sure if she was putting on an act for Mr. Silverstein or if she was just scared to face him.

When she got in the car I said, "Girl, what's wrong with you?"

"I didn't sleep all night. I'm so nervous to face Mr. Silverstein."

"Have you thought about what you're gonna say?" "There's nothing to say but the truth, and the truth isn't going to help me." We all were quiet on the ride to let Betty get her mind right.

When we walked into the office, Mr. Silverstein was already there. He immediately went in.

"Betty, why were you not at work yesterday?" Betty was frozen. She didn't answer. He asked her again but this time a little firmer, "Betty, why were you not at work

yesterday?" *Momma always would say that you know the s**t is coming cause the fart will give it away... well the s**t was coming!*

Betty said, "Because I went home to see my family just like Clara!"

"We discussed that you were not given the day off like Clara and that you needed to be here to open the office!" He continued, "In eighteen years, my office has never been closed the day after Christmas, and I can only imagine the business that we lost!" Mr. Silverstein was visibly upset.

Then Betty said, "Well then Clara should have been here to work too. I have more time on the job than her."

I gave Betty a look that she was going too far. That's when Mr. Silverstein looked like he was pissed!

"You are not the boss and you don't make those decisions! If you are not happy with the way I'm doing things here, you're free to look for another job!" I tried to jump in and calm things down.

I said, "Okay, let's all calm down-," and before I could finish, Betty cut me off and said, "Maybe I will! Since you don't seem to appreciate all the work that I've done for the past two years and all you can seem to think about is what it would be like to f**ck my sister, I will find another job!" Mr. Silverstein was beet red in the face.

"Betty you are fired! Get your things and get out now!"

Betty grabbed a few of her belongings, then she

turned to me and said, "Clara, bring all my things home tonight. I don't want to be in this place another minute!" She swung the door open and left.

I couldn't believe what had just happened. I told Mr. Silverstein that I had to go check on my sister and that I'd be right back. When I finally caught up to Betty, she was headed to the trolley and she was smiling.

"Girl, why are you smiling after all that?"

"Because I got to give his ole dirty ass a piece of my mind!"

"But what are you going to do now?"

"Girl, I'm not worried. I'll get another job but I'm not going to let anyone treat me unfairly! You go on back in there and make sure he's not having a heart attack. I'll see you later at the house." I hugged and kissed her and headed back to the office.

When I got back, Mr. Silverstein was popping aspirin and drinking Scotch. He started rambling.

"Can you believe that she would talk to me like that after all that I've done for her?" He went on and on for about thirty minutes before he realized that he was talking about my sister. He apologized for ranting for so long and told me that he appreciated me and that he wanted me to stay on. In my heart, I knew that he was treating Betty different than me and that this was my chance to say something about it. I said, "Mr. Siverstein, I'd like to be able to speak my mind to you." He agreed and gave his permission.

I started by saying, "Some of the things that Betty said was true. You do treat me better in some ways than you do her, and she has been here longer and she trained me." I told him how hurt her feelings were that we were all going home and that she would have been by herself on Christmas. I told him how much she loved her job and how much respect she had for him. Once I finished talking you could tell that I had struck a chord. He asked me to call Betty and have her come to the office the next morning so they could talk. The rest of the day we worked in silence, I guess he needed some time to think things through.

When I got to the house later on that evening, Betty had cooked, cleaned, and baked a cake.

I asked, "What got into you?"

She said, "This is all for you!" She sat me down and said, "I really appreciate what you did for me with Mr. Silverstein. A lot of people would just look out for themselves and I want to say thank you and I love you!"

"You are my sister Betty and I appreciate that you got me the job, and that you, Mally, and Gladys gave me a chance to come to Philly and make a better life for me and my children. I'm never going to forget that. Anything I can do to help y'all, I'm gonna always do it." We hugged and went in the kitchen to eat some of this good ole meal she made.

Soon after, everything was back to normal at work

between Mr. Silverstein and Betty and I could breath
easy. He still treated me a little special, but nobody paid
him any mind. It seemed like months had passed and
everyone was getting along, the business was growing,
and we were getting more customers because another
insurance company around the corner closed down.

CHAPTER 18

I'm Tryin To Keep My Promises

I WAS DOING REAL GOOD KEEPING TWO OUT OF THE THREE promises I made to God. I went to National Temple Baptist Church every Sunday. I sent Momma money every week. Only thing was, I hadn't been back to Hustle in six months. Cicely was writing us letters every week asking when she could come for a visit so I finally sat Gladys, Mally, and Betty down and asked when we were gonna let Cicely come up. We had promised her when were in Hustle for Christmas. We all agreed that she could come the next month. Betty said that this was good timing cause her and Burt was going to be getting a place together in a few months cause she was pregnant and getting married. We were so happy for her! Burt was a good man and had a good job with the phone company and he loved himself some Betty.

I wrote Cicely and told her that she could come up the next month. It seemed like I got her letter back the next week with all her arrangements and time that the Greyhoud would get to Philly. I remembered how excited I was when I was getting ready to visit. And just like

me, I knew this wasn't just a regular visit. That girl was not going back any time soon either. When James and me went down to Filbert Street to get her from the bus station, all I could think about was Momma and having the burden of all those children.

She still had Ernestine and Carrie there to help her out, and if Cicely got a decent job, she could send more money home to really help out.

When Cicely stepped down off the bus, instead of looking excited, she looked scared to death. She was clutching her bag real close to her chest and looking all round like she was lost.

"Cicely, over here!" She looked around and when she saw us, she looked like she seen Jesus. She came running over and said, "Lord, I ain't never seen such tall buildings and peoples and cars movin so fast!"

We hugged and said, "Welcome to Philly! Girl you haven't seen a thing. Wait until you see the trolley train that runs right in the middle of the street!"

"What in the devil is a trolley?" At that moment, one was coming up Market Street. She stared at it and said, "This city life is gonna take some gettin use to, but I's ready!"

When we got to the house, she reminded me of myself when I first got to the city. She couldn't believe that we had such a nice place with nice furniture and stuff. I have to give all the thanks to Gladys, Mally, and Betty cause all that stuff was there when I came. They

really made a good life for themselves and now us.

Cicely was ready to go out and hit the streets. She was asking when we was goin out and where was all our men friends. Even though we were tired, we all knew how bad we wanted to go out when we first got here so we planned to take her to Jake's Place. James was pickin us up at nine o'clock. Jake's was a new lounge in town that had been open for a couple of months now so everybody came out on Saturday nights. It stayed open til 2:00 a.m., had a live band, and they served soul food til 1:00 a.m. They said some Italian man that loved black people owned it.

I knew how fast I got a man when I moved to Philly, and from the way Cicely looked, it wasn't going to be a problem for her to get one too. Cicely was beautiful with big titties, hips and butt and a tiny waist. She had brown skin and silky long black hair. She looked more like Momma than any of us and had those strong Indian features. Back in Hustle, the boys and men always did like Cicely. The rest of us would get the ones she didn't want.

When we got to Jake's, just like I thought, all the men were looking at her and trying to talk to her. They were asking me, Betty, and Gladys who she was, just like when I first came to town. It seemed like all the men wanted to be our friends and the women wished they could kill us and chop us up in a pot of greens. Men were buying us drinks left and right and Cicely was out on the dance floor dancing with everybody there. You could tell she was having a good time. We were all having a good time.

The band was jamming, and I was so into the music that I didn't notice that James was over in the corner having some words with some woman. When I looked closer, it was the same lady that was in the restaurant a few months back. When I walked over, I saw that the woman wasn't looking too happy.

"James is everything alright over here?"

Before he could answer me she said, "No, it ain't! James is my daughter's daddy and he's acting like he don't know me now cause he's with you!"

James said, "Clara, go back and enjoy the band. Let me handle this and I'll explain everything later."

From the look in his eyes, I knew this wasn't the time to ask questions so I did as he asked and walked away.

She said, "Go on and walk off like you didn't hear what I said. You'll be next. As soon as a new piece of ass comes around, you'll be thrown to the side too!"

I tried to act like what she was saying wasn't bothering me, but my stomach was in knots. I looked back at her and rolled my eyes. Was the man I was in love with really a no-good dog just like the men in Hustle?

James talked to her for about five more minutes before coming over and asking me to talk to him outside. When we got outside he said, "That woman that I was talking to is crazy. I went out with her a couple of times and we f**ked one time and she is trying to say that I'm her kid's father! I know that I didn't cum in that girl cause I knew she was fast. I need you to believe me. If I thought

for a second I was that girl's daddy, I would take care of her. This lady is looking for much more. She wants me to marry her and give the kid my last name, cause her mother and father are pressuring her. I'm not doing it!"

I pulled him close and wrapped my arms around his neck and said, "I believe you James. You say you're not the daddy, then I'm gonna stand by you."

He hugged me tightly and said, "Clara, I love you!"

"I love you too!" We stood outside for about five more minutes just kissing and hugging. I was so in love with this man!

When we finally went back inside, I saw Cicely sitting at the bar having a drink with this older white man. When we walked over to her she said, "Hey Clara, girl I been lookin for you all night! This is Jake, he own this place! Jake, this my sista Clara and her boyfriend James." We all shook hands.

Jake said, "Cicely tells me that she just moved here from Virginia. How long have you lived in Philly?"

James answered and said that he lived here for the past fourteen years. I told him I'd been here for a little over two years.

He was impressed that we had moved to Philly to make a better life for our family given our age. It was easy to tell that he liked Cicely. I knew it wouldn't be long before she had a man and she could have had any of the ones up in Jake's. Cicely was looking for a certain type of man, and that meant one that had a lot of money to

spend. She came to Philly with a plan and she was going to work it.

Jake gave us free drinks all night. After he closed the place at 2:00 a.m., he had the cook make us all kinds of food. We didn't leave out of there until 4:00 a.m. I never ate and drank so much in all my life. My head was spinning and so was everything else. By the time we finally got to the house, it was nearly 5:00 a.m. I told James to just come and sleep on the couch cause we weren't in any shape to drive to his house and I had to be at church by 11:00 a.m.

I swear, as soon as I laid my head down, it was ten o'clock and time to get ready for church. Everybody else had already told me they weren't going, so it was just me that had to get ready! I had made a promise to God and this was one promise I was going to keep. So, I left everybody sleeping and went on to church.

CHAPTER 19

Cicely Is Jake's New Woman

CICELY HIT IT BIG! EVER SINCE THAT NIGHT AT THE CLUB, she has been hanging out with Jake. She would come by the house for a few minutes to grab some things then she was off to somewhere with Jake. One evening, she came by and told us that she wanted us to come to Jake's that Saturday night. She had a surprise for us. It had only been a few weeks and she was already working at Jake's place as the new manager. He got her a new apartment in Center City with all this fancy furniture. She had a closet full of new dresses, purses, hats, coats, and scarfs. It was like she was a rich white woman.

Jake really took a liking to Cicely. Word on the street was that he owned a lot of houses in Philly that he rented to colored people and they said he was in the Mafia too. I didn't really know what that meant, but I guess the Mafia in Philly is like the KKK in Hustle. Anyway, he had never been married and he only dated pretty colored women and would give them a real nice life. Cicely told us that he gave her $50 and told her to mail it to Momma and tell her that she wasn't coming back right now and she would

be sending more money next week. I bet when Momma got that letter and saw all that money she was thinking, *all this money, you ain't never got to send her ass back! Just keep the money coming!* I laughed to myself picturing her.

A few weeks had gone by and one night, Cicely came over to the house. She looked so fancy, I barely knew who she was. She had on a new dress, shoes, and purse. Her hair was all done up and she had her face all made up. She could have given Dorothy Dandridge a run for her money. She had on pearl earrings with the necklace and bracelet to match. She was telling us all about her new place. All the houses in Center City were real nice. Me and James would ride down there some Saturdays just looking at them. It was only a few coloreds that lived in Center City and they were doctors and lawyers. This girl must have put it on Jake's ass!

She asked James to take us to see her new place. We were all excited to see it so we jumped in the car and headed downtown. When we got there, it was a big ole fancy brick building with a white man that opened the door for us. When she went in, he nodded his head and said, "Good evening, Ms. Fortune." We looked at each other in shock! When we got off the elevator, I was feeling a little woozy because that was my first time on one.

Cicely's new place was out of this world! I'd never imagined the kind of stuff she had. I hadn't even seen this kind of furniture in the Sears & Roebucks catalog, and they had some fancy stuff. We jumped up and down like

kids in a candy store.

I said, "Girl, didn't I tell you, you were gonna love Philly!"

Cicely said, "I ain't know it was this good! Girl, Jake treats me so nice, like I'm a queen or somethin! His d**k a little small for my likin but all the gifts and stuff make up for it!"

We laughed so long our stomachs were hurting.

Betty said, "You better act like it's big and you love it, cause men like this don't come around too often!"

James said, "Alright now, I don't want to hear all that!"

Gladys was walking around with her mouth open like she couldn't believe that this was really Cicely's new place. Mally was at work as usual and missed out on all of the fun and Fanny wa always with her white boyfriend. I hadn't seen her in almost 5 months. She would call every now and again but that was it.

We all sat around for a couple of hours. She told us all about her plans for Jake's spot, how they were going to bring some real singers and bands in to make the place jump. She kept telling us to make sure we were at Jake's by nine o'clock on Saturday because she had a big surprise for us. We kept asking her what it was but she wouldn't tell us.

All the way home, we talked about Cicely's new place, her new job, and of course, Jake. We were all real happy for her and our family cause the Fortune girls were

about to take over Philly—it was time to Hustle!

Seemed like the week flew by. We were back and forth at Cicely's place because she didn't like staying there alone and Jake didn't stay there every night. James was getting mad because he was used to me staying with him and he didn't like how we were always hanging at Cicely's house. I could tell he was a bit jealous.

We stayed at Cicely's house that Friday night too, cause we all had hairdresser appointments Saturday morning in the city. Betty and me got up early and cooked everybody breakfast. Right after our hair appointments, Cicely took everybody shopping for new dresses that we was all wearing to Jake's that night. We could not believe we were up in all these fancy places that we had one time only dreamed of. Unlike us, Cicely acted like she belonged. Most of the time, the shop workers thought I was a white woman taking out my help, but then when Cicely would whip out the money to pay, they knew then that a colored woman was in charge.

I always hated that people thought I was white because I was proud to be colored. But what I learned was that people were gonna think what they wanted to anyway, so it wasn't any use trying to change their minds. If they thought I was white and it helped me further along, then I'll be white.

After all our hair was done, Cicely said she wanted to go to this dress store named Priscilla's, it was the nicest dress store in the city. I don't even know if colored women

shopped there but Cicely didn't care. She said that's where Jake told her to go for dresses. I was sure nuff right though. When we walked in, the lady looked like she wanted to call the police. She acted like she was scared to death.

"Can I help you ladies with something?"

Cicely said, "Yes, I want to buy five dresses. Can you show us some?"

Like a snob, the lady said, "Our dresses are very expensive, and we-," before she could finish, Cicely said, "I ain't ask how expensive they is. I asked you to show us some!" The lady turned red, and went to go get dresses. We all looked at each other and bust out laughing.

When she came back, she had the prettiest dresses that I'd ever seen. We each picked one and went to try them on. We each loved the dress we'd picked and Cicely had them bring out an extra one.

"I want all of them!"

When the lady said they were $12 each, I nearly passed out. Cicely just counted out the cash and paid her. Now, the lady was being extra friendly and telling us to come back again. Money sure does make people act different. Cicely told us she had some running around to do with Jake and that she would see us later that night. We all hugged and headed home.

When we got to the house, James was there and he didn't look too happy. I leaned over to give him a kiss and he moved his head.

"What's wrong with you?"

"Ever since your sister came in town and start fooling around with Jake, you don't have no time for me!"

"Look, I like spending time with you. But I like spending time with my sisters too. She's only been in town a few weeks."

"You never spent that much time with Betty, Gladys, or Mally. Is it because Cicely has all this money and fancy stuff and so that's what has your nose open?"

"My daddy died a long time ago and I left my husband in Virginia, so it's been a long time since I answered to a man and I ain't gonna start now! If you have a problem with me hanging with my sisters, then that's your problem and not mine!" He got up and headed for the door and when he was out, I slammed it behind him just like Poppa use to do.

When they heard the door slam, Gladys and Mally came from upstairs and asked what happened. I told them that James is acting like an ass so he left.

Gladys said, "Girl, let's get ready for tonight. We don't have time to be worrying about James."

When 8:30p.m. rolled around, we were all dressed and looking good. It's a shame that James and me was at odds cause now we had to catch the trolley. You should have seen the way all the people on the trolley was staring at us. I'm sure they had never seen no ladies as fine as we were on no damn trolley.

When we walked in Jake's, all the heads turned in our direction. It was like somebody had stopped the

music. Men and women followed us with their eyes as we walked over to our table. When Cicely saw us, she came over with a bottle of whiskey. I've never seen so many jealous women, so many mean looks.

Gladys said, "Do y'all see all these women giving us the evil eye?"

Cicely said, "Don't pay them heffas no mind. They is jealous!" She said it loud enough so they could hear and she looked at them and rolled her eyes. Then she said, "I know nobody don't want a good ole down home Virginia ass whoopin!"

Every woman that heard what she said turned and looked the other way.

"We ain't payin these simple girls no mind. I told y'all I had a surprise and I just need five more minutes. I'll be right back," said Cicely. She went off into the backroom we didn't pay her any mind and started to enjoy the whiskey she brought to the table.

About ten minutes went by and we saw Cicely and some girl heading over to us.

Gladys asked, "Who is that girl with Cicely?"

"I don't know but she sure does favor Ernestine," said Mally.

I looked closer and said, "Lord, that is Ernestine!"

When they got over to us and we knew for sure it was her, we jumped up and down screaming. She looked stunning! Her hair was all done up and she had on make up and that other dress that Cicely had bought from

Priscilla's. Now we knew why Cicely asked for five dresses. We couldn't believe it. Cicely had planned everything. She promised Ernestine that when she got on her feet in Philly, she was going to send for her. Nobody knew it was going to be that fast.

Cicely told us that she wrote Momma and told her to let Ernestine come up here and work and with all the money that we were gonna be sending, that she ain't have to work no more and she could just watch the children. I think Jake sending that $50 had a lot to do with Momma going along with everything.

It felt good being with all of my sisters and we were just living out our dreams of coming to Philly and making a better life for ourselves. We were on our way! We made a toast, "To the Fortune girls!"

We partied until the last person left at 2:00 a.m. We were all so drunk that Jake had one of his friends take us down to Cicely's place. I was missing having James around to always give us a ride.

CHAPTER 20

Mr. Silverstein Makes His Move

IT'S NOTHING NEW THAT ON SUNDAY MORNING, EVERBODY was hung over and nobody was going to church but me. I asked every last one of them to get up and go to church and they all acted like they couldn't hear me. I got myself together and put on one of Cicely's outfits. It was a little fancy for church, but I couldn't wear what I had on last night with the whiskey and smoke scents in it.

When I got downstairs, James was sitting in the front of the building in his car. When he saw me walk out, he got out and started walking over to me. I tried to act like I didn't see him and walked in the other direction.

"Clara, let me talk to you for a minute," he said as he gently grabbed my arm. "I came to Jake's last night, cause I figured you'd need a ride home. But then I saw one of Jake's friends was giving y'all a ride. Y'all looked so beautiful. I just came and sat out here all night cause I knew you were gonna need a ride to church this morning."

"That was mighty sweet of you."

"Clara, I'm sorry for the way that I acted the other day and I miss you. I'd rather share you with your sisters

than not see you at all."

He didn't have to say another word. I hugged him around his neck and kissed him. This was my man and I loved him. We spent all Sunday together, he went to church with me and then we went and got something to eat. After that we went back to his house and made love for the rest of the day.

The next day, Betty was having morning sickness so she didn't come in to work. Mr. Silverstein was in a real good mood. He went out and bought coffee and bagels for breakfast. All day he kept acting funny, he was smiling and humming all around the office. Then, he finally bust out and said, "Clara, you know that I like you!"

I almost fell out my chair. I didn't know what to say so I said, "I like you too, Mr. Silverstein."

"No. I like you," he smiled and lifted his eyebrows up and down, like how people would do when they were trying to be fresh.

"Well, Mr. Silverstein, you're married and I have a boyfriend."

"Clara, I know all that and I'm not looking for a sexual relationship. I just think you're a beautiful woman and I'd like to help you. We can spend some time outside of work, a man my age can't want much more." He smiled and just looked at me real innocent.

Mr. Silverstein had to be in his early sixties, he wasn't a bad looking man at all. He was just white. I had never liked a white man before. So, I never answered him. I just

kept doing my work.

All day I kept thinking about what he'd said to me. What did that mean? I think Mr. Silverstein knew he made me uncomfortable because he didn't say too much the rest of the day. I tried not to act funny but I just couldn't believe that he was sweet on me. When James picked me up from work, he could tell that something was on my mind. I just told him that I missed Momma and the kids. But my mind was wondering about why Mr. Silvestein wanted to help me and wasn't looking for sex in return. Something didn't sound right to me, so I told Betty and them what he said.

When I told them, Mally said, "Sometimes when men get a certain age, they like to be around young women cause it makes them feel young. A lot of times it's not about sex."

Then Betty said, "Girl are you crazy! That's your boss and he's married!"

Mally said, "He said he doesn't want sex!"

Gladys said, "That's what they all say in the beginning!"

I jumped in and said, "Well, I'm not having sex with Mr. Silverstein. I don't care what he wants." I told them I would talk to him about it in the morning.

Betty wasn't coming in again, so the first thing I did when I got to work the next morning was to ask to speak to Mr. Silverstein.

Before I could even talk, he started, "Clara, I know

why you want to talk me. I apologize for the way I spoke to you yesterday. I've just been having so many problems. My wife has just been diagnosed with cancer…" and he just began crying and saying how sorry he was! I got up and got him some tissue and told him that I accepted his apology and that if he was just looking for a friend to talk to that we could be friends. For some reason, I felt sorry for him. He always seemed like a nice man, all the customers liked him, and he was always respectful to colored people.

From that day on, Mr. Silverstein talked to me about everything. He told me that if I was ever gonna get my children and mother up to Philly, I needed to be a home owner. I had never given any thought to owning my own home. He started telling me how much money to save and what kind of accounts to put the money in to grow the interest. When I would go in the bank talking to those white folks about certificate of deposits and savings bonds, they'd look at me confused and wondering how I knew all that stuff. He really taught me a lot.

CHAPTER 21

Ernestine Is Fittin Right In

ERNESTINE DIDN'T WASTE ANY TIME GETTING A JOB. SHE got a job within a week at Horn & Harderts Resturant in center city working as a waitress. It was a high-end restaurant where only white folks ate. She was staying with Cicely so she could walk there in five minutes and she worked up at Jake's when she wasn't working at the restaurant. She wasn't one to run the streets. She came to Philly to work and make some money and that's what she was doing.

Ernestine was going to be working at Jake's on the Saturday night that Randy Newton and his band was playing. They were the best group in Philly so the place was going to be packed! We were all looking forward to going because we hadn't seen much of Cicely since she was working all the time. Betty and Burt had moved in together and were expecting their first child. Mally was always with her man or at work and Gladys worked a lot too and of course Fanny was nowhere to be found. It was like everybody was off doing their own thing.

Ernestine always stayed to herself as a kid. She

would play and talk to herself all the time. Nobody was surprised that she was acting the same way now that she was here. She would work day and night and had started seeing an older gentleman named Norman Jefferson. With all of the men that were interested in her, we didn't understand why she liked this ole ass man that could be her Poppa but she was always strange.

After only a couple of months, Ernestine and Jeff, as we called him, was talking about getting a place together. She seemed to like him even though he was thirty years older than her. He really didn't come around us much so we didn't know much about him. A few weeks after they moved in together, Ernestine invited us over to her new place for dinner. They lived a few blocks from Jake's place in West Philly on Holly Street. Their place was a really cute three-bedroom row home with a little stoop. They even had bought some nice furniture for the living room and kitchen. Ernestine told us that Jeff was going to help her bring Butchie Boy and Cicely to Philly in the next six months and they were gonna get married. We were all excited for her but thought she was moving a little too fast. She had just met this man. Anyway, we all enjoyed the evening laughing, drinking, and talking trash.

When me and James was driving home later that night, he told me that he knew someone that knew Jeff and that he had another family. I was shocked and wondered if Ernestine knew. James asked me not to say anything until he was sure. I promised that I wouldn't say

a thing to Ernestine, but that I had to tell my sisters. He was okay with that but that they couldn't say anything either until he knew for sure.

After a few days, James came back and confirmed that it was true that Jeff was married and had five children with his wife, and that his wife was blind. What kind of no-good man would leave his blind wife and children? There was no way that Ernestine knew this. After I told Betty and them what James told me, we decided that she needed to know. We asked her to meet us at Jake's and when we started to tell her, she cut us off and said she already knew and they were not together no more. She said that Jeff told her in the very beginning and that she met his oldest two daughters Marjorie and Ditty.

We asked Ernestine, why she wanted to be with a man that's three times her age and already had a family?

"Age is only a number and I need somebody that wanna help me and help me get my chilren up from the country. He the first man that ever offered to help me." She went on to say, "When we first met and I told him that I had a little boy and gal, he promised that he would be sure that they get up to Philly. What man y'all know care bout some other man chilren being wit they momma?"

We all sat there quiet while she went on and on about what a good man Jeff was. She told us that his wife was always cheatin on him and always had other mens up in the house while he was at work and the chilren use to tell.

I said, "Well, James said she was blind."

Ernestine said, "You don't need to see to the d**k, you just need to feel it!"

We fell out laughing, but in the back of my mind I didn't trust him. He's too damn old to be with my baby sister.

After awhile, we all agreed that if she liked it, we loved it. Ernestine was always stubborn and walked to the beat of her own drum and everybody has to do what's best for them.

CHAPTER 22

James Ain't Who I Thought He Was

I 'D BEEN DATING JAMES FOR GOING ON THREE YEARS NOW and he was never at a job. Every time I asked him about what he does to make money, he'd change the subject or say, "A little of this or a little of that." I didn't really know what that meant but he always dressed nice, had a nice home and car, and he bought me nice gifts but he never went to work.

One day, I said to him, "James, we've been together for almost three years and I told you everything about me and I don't feel like I know everything about you."

"What do you feel that you don't know?"

"Well first off, whatever happened with that lady that said you were her child's father?"

"I told you that I wasn't, that we slept together one time and she tried to say that I'm the father."

"Well, you do know that it only takes one time to make a child."

"Yes, I know that, but something in my gut says that child isn't mine."

"Have you seen the child? Does she look like you?"

"No, and I don't plan on it!" I could tell he was getting agitated so I said, "And another thing, I don't know where you work! People be asking me what my boyfriend does for a living and I look silly cause I don't know."

"Clara some things are better that you don't know." He kissed my forehead, and I knew that was the end of the questions. "Now what does the prettiest girl in Philly want for lunch?" The way he answered that last question had my stomach in knots. I had lost my appetite but I tried not to let him know and said, "Let's get some seafood from down in the bottom!"

The bottom was what we called West Philly around where Ernestine and Jeff lived. They had a lot of colore-downed businesses and restaurants. Colored folks didn't go into center city to eat, that's where white people went. The food wasn't as good and it was much more expensive than in the bottom. The only time we ate or shopped down there is when Cicely was treating us on Jake's dime.

Once we got to Tootsie's and was about to walk in, James said, "Clara, go on inside and get us a seat. I'll be right in."

He had that serious look again so I didn't ask any questions. I didn't go right in and instead stood in the corner to see what was going on. At first, I thought it might be one of those women again acting a fool, but I watched as James walked over to a man. They were talking and it looked like the man was getting a little nervous. Next thing I know, James was punching the man until his

face was bloody and the man was knocked out cold! I'd never seen James that mad before.

He yelled and told the man, "DO NOT PLAY WITH MY MONEY NIGGA! I WILL KILL YOUR ASS!" He pulled out a handkerchief and started wiping the blood off his hands. Then he threw the handkerchief on the man and said, "HAVE MY MONEY BY TONIGHT!"

During the whole situation, people had been screaming and running. James turned around and walked back towards Tootsie's.

I was a nervous wreck but I hurried and sat down and tried to act like I hadn't seen what had just happened. He went to the toilet first, so this gave me a little more time to get myself together. By the time he got to the table, I didn't think I'd be able to hide it so when he sat down I asked, "Another baby momma?"

He chuckled and said, "Not quite. What you eating?"

I couldn't believe what I just saw and now he's acting like nothing happened. Who was the man that I fell in love with?

I did my best to pretend like nothing was wrong but I couldn't get the image of him beating that man out of my mind. I acted like the food made my stomach upset and that I needed to go home and lay down. I asked him to take me home since I hadn't seen my sisters in a few days.

When I got there, nobody was home. James told me he had some business to handle and that he'd be back.

This gave me more time to get myself together. *What kind of sh*t is this nigga into? Am I safe? If he's around here beating people up like that, is someone going to come and try to get back at him and I'm in the middle?* I couldn't wait for Mally or somebody to come to the house. I waited for hours and nobody came, so I got my stuff and caught the trolley to Jake's. I knew Cicely would be there.

When I got there, she said, "Girl, what in the world wrong wit you? You look like you done seen a ghost!"

I said, "Girl, I don't think I know James. We was in the bottom and he beat this man until he was bloody and knocked out. Then he came in Tootsie's and ate like nothing happened!"

Cicely said, "He beat a man bloody?"

That's when Jake said, "He probably owed him money." He said it so calmly that we looked at him like he was crazy?

I said, "Owed him money? Owed him money for what?"

He said, "Sweetheart, you didn't know that you were dating the numbers man?"

"The numbers man? What's that?"

"You girls really are from the country!" He laughed and said, "The numbers man takes all of the bets that people place on sports, races, boxing matches and so on. How do you think he makes his money?"

I must have looked shocked cause he said, "I thought you knew. Sometimes people don't pay and when that

happens, you have to make an example out of them. Did he do it out in the open?"

I said, "Yes, right on Lancaster Ave at twelve o'clock midday!"

He chuckled and said, "Message sent!"

Now everything was starting to make sense. This is why every time I asked about his job, he would change the subject or say that I didn't need to know. I was so mad that James didn't tell me that he was the numbers man! What if somebody knew I was his lady and tried to hurt me? He should have told me!

After I calmed down, I took the trolley back home to wait for James. When I got there, he was sitting in the car waiting for me. He could tell that I was mad cause I was red like fire and walking like I was in a race!

Before I could get in the house and he could say hello, I said, "Why you didn't tell me you're the numbers man? I saw the way you beat that man bloody today! What if somebody tried to hurt me cause of what you do? You are a liar and I don't know who you are!"

I was yelling so loud that people start coming on their porch and looking out the window. He tried to grab me and I pulled away.

He grabbed me firm and said, "Lower your voice. You have all these people looking at us. Go in the house and I'll explain everything."

I pulled away and said, "No, you ain't coming in my house!"

He grabbed me by the arm and walked me towards the door so firm I couldn't get loose. I was trying to pull away and I said, "Oh what? You gonna beat me bloody like you did that man?"

He whispered in my ear and said real deep and slowly, "Clara, I'm not gonna ask you again to lower your voice and go in the house."

The way his voice sounded and his eyes looked, I knew he meant business so I went on in the house to see what this fool had to say.

When we got inside, he pushed me on the couch and he started talking.

"Do you want these folks to call the police on me? You out here yelling and actin all crazy!"

He was walking back and forth real fast and he looked pissy mad.

"I don't let no one get close to me. I didn't tell you because the less you know the better you are. I try to keep my business and personal life separate. What you saw today is the ugly side of the business and it doesn't happen a lot, but sometimes it's necessary in this line of work."

He came and sat down on the couch, still angry. He got up in my face and looked me right in my eyes. "Now that you know you have a choice to make. This is what I do and you need to decide if you want to stay or leave. The choice is yours."

I didn't know what to say. He wasn't normally like this and in almost three years, this was the first time that I

ever saw this side of him. I thought about it for a minute.

"I'm gonna stay with you but I don't ever want to be around nothing like that again."

He was still looking me dead in my eyes and said, "I promise that as long as I live, you NEVER have to worry about anything like that happening around you again!" He kissed me on the forehead, which meant we were done talking about it. I can't lie, I was still a little scared.

CHAPTER 23

Come Get Y'all Chilrens

WE GOT A LETTER FROM HAMILTON AND HE SAID THAT sh*t was getting real bad in Hustle.

Hey Sistas!
I hope y'all is well! Y'all gonna have to come home and get y'all chilren! Benji, Elleeboo, and even little Butchie Boy is giving Ms. Rosie a bunch of trouble. They was in town stealing from Luke Harper's store and even set fire to a barn on John Daniel's farm. The Sheriff been out to the farm like three times in the last week. Ms. Rosie been cryin herself sick. He said if he come back one more time, he gonna lock they Black asses up and they gonna be ole as him 'fore they see the light of day! They don't listen to a word Ms. Rosie say and they don't listen to me either! I told them I was gonna take my strap to them and they told me that if I tried, it would be the last time that I took a strap to anybody! Lord knows I don't want to kill none of y'all chilren, but you know I will! They is down right demons!
Walter May is drinkin hisself crazy and breakin up everthang in the house when he get mad at Ms. Rosie cause

she won't give him no money for whiskey.

Carrie runnin around wit drunk ass Robbie Reynolds and he whippin her ass every time he get drunk. I hate to have to tell you this in a letter, but lil Cicely done lost half her finger in a bicycle accident! She was running chasing Carrie while she was ridin and somehow her finger got caught up in the chain. Dr. Berger tried to sew it back on, but it wasn't cleaned right and gang green set in so they had to cut it off. They took her to the hospital in Richmond to have it done, so she had good care but poor lil thang only got half of her pointing finger on her right hand. She look right pitiful but she still the prettiest lil black gal I seen!

Ms. Rosie can't take much more. Juanita do help take care of lil Cicely but she gettin right sassy to and she sneakin up the road to see Ryan O'Neil, one of them Wood boys. So y'all need to get on back to the country and gets y'all chilren!

Your Brother,
Hamilton

When we read the letter, Ernestine bust out crying and said she was going to get her chilren in two weeks. Cicely and me weren't ready to bring our children to Philly. Where were they going to stay? We didn't have a place big enough for our children. We needed more than two weeks to make plans to bring them up here. Ernestine and Jeff had already started their plans on getting Butchie Boy and Lil Cicely, now this just gave them more reason.

Those two weeks went by quick. Cicely and me still hadn't figured out a place for our children to go so we let Ernestine go to pick up her children and we sent some money, clothes, and food for Momma until we could figure something out.

Ernestine and Jeff stayed down in the country for a week before they came back with Butchie and Lil Cicely. She told us that while she was home, she saw Cathy. She said that Cathy wants to come and visit and she's going to leave Paulie and the kids at home and come stay with her and Jeff for a week. I was excited cause Cathy was pretty, smart, and funny as heck. I knew Ernestine was excited too cause her and Cathy was real close growing up.

Ernestine and Jeff wasn't a bit more ready to bring those children to Philly than the man on the moon. They said the children and everybody in the house pitched a fit when it was time for them to leave. Momma was crying, Butchie Boy and lil Cicely was holding on to her leg and Momma was holding on to them. She was cussing Hamilton out for writing us and telling us to come get the children. They said she called him every name under the sun!

Ernestine and Jeff said the children cried all the way up the road until they fell asleep and then when they woke up, they cried some more. They looked right pitiful when I saw them. They wouldn't eat or play, just sat there looking at each other asking when they was going back to Momma's house. I didn't realize how attached they

were to Momma and how hurtful it was going to be for the children to leave her. She was the only Momma they knew.

CHAPTER 24

Cathy Is Coming To Visit

THE VERY NEXT WEEK AFTER ERNESTINE AND JEFF CAME back with the kids, we all went down to the bus station to meet Cathy. I guess you could say that she was everyone's favorite sister. Before we could see her get off the bus we could hear her yelling, "Where is y'all at cause Cathy is in town and Philly ain't never gonna be the same again!"

She stepped from behind some fat white man and we all screamed and ran and hugged her. After about five minutes of hugging and jumping up and down, we were ready to make it to Jeff and Ernestine's house. Cathy looked great. It had been almost two years since I last seen her. She filled us in on all that was going on in the country. "When is y'all gon come get your bad ass chilren for they kill my Momma?"

Cicely and me said that we were looking into making some plans. She said that Benji and Elleeboo were running amuck in Hustle. She didn't know what had got into them but that Momma was gettin tired. She said the younger ones wasn't really a problem and that

Momma was so hurt when they left, but that she really needed some help with those older boys. We knew we had to get them out the country before they ended up in jail or dead.

Of course, Cathy was ready to hit the town. She was full of energy and raring to go. After she filled us in, she said tonight wasn't the night to think about that cause we were all going out! Cicely had already told Jake that Cathy was coming to town and that this was going to be a special night cause all the sisters were gonna be there except Fanny. We took the trolley with them down to the bottom then Cicely and me left to go get ready for the night. We went back to Cicely's house to get dressed. On the way there, we talked about what we were going do to get those boys up here to Philly.

I told her that Mr. Silvestein had been talking to me about buying a house. I told her that we could put our money together and get a house. Cicely wasn't too sure on what her plans were but she knew that she didn't want to own no house in Philly. I knew then that this was something I was going to have to do on my own.

Later that night when we got to Jake's, Cathy, Jeff, and Ernestine were already there. We had a section that Jake had set up for us with all kinds of whiskey and food. James came in a little later with one of his friends. He introduced us and said that her name was Bea, but she dressed and acted like a man. I pulled James to the side and whispered in his ear.

"Is she a man or a woman?"

"She's a woman that like women," he said and gave me a funny look.

I couldn't stop looking at her. I had never met a real one of them kind of people. I had always heard about them, but had never seen one with my own eyes and if they was rumored to be that way, whether they was a man or woman, they tried to hide it. Bea was different. It didn't seem like she cared. She was a pretty woman with wavy hair, but she kept it short like a man. She didn't wear any makeup or lipstick and had on pants like a man too. I think I was staring so much because there sure was a lot of real women talking to her and flirting with her. I guess they knew and were okay with it.

Anyway, we danced, ate, and drank way into the morning. By 2:00 a.m., we were all drunk, tired, and ready to go home. I had to get up in a few hours for church. I knew the rest of them heathens weren't going, so I told James that I was ready to go. With all the dancing and drinking we were doing, I didn't notice that Cathy and Bea was over in the corner sitting kind of close. Bea had her arm around Cathy and she was sitting up under her. It shocked me cause I knew Cathy didn't have a clue that she was a woman, cause she looked like a very nice looking man.

I yelled over and said, "Hey Cathy, come here for a minute." She got up from the table with Bea and headed over. I couldn't tell what she said, but I could tell that she

liked her.

The way she was looking at her told me for sure she didn't know Bea was a woman. When Cathy came over, I said, "Girl, don't you know that she's one of them funny women that like other women?"

"Yea girl, and she is fine!" She was peeking around me looking over at Bea waving.

I looked over and Bea was waving back. I nearly fell to the floor!

"What you think, cause I live in the country ain't no womens like that down there? Girl, things changing!" I was shocked. "I like womens and mens!" I nearly fell on the floor again.

"Am I drunk or did you just say you like women?"

"You heard me right. I like womens and I'm goin home wit that one tonight!" Then she blew Bea a kiss.

This girl was about to give me a heart attack. She hugged me and said goodnight and went on back to where Bea was and the next thing I knew, she was leaving with her.

As me and James rode to his house, I had a thousand questions about Bea.

"How you know Bea?"

"She works with me in the numbers game."

"Has she always been funny?"

"If you mean has she always liked women, yes."

"How long have you known her and is my sister gonna be safe with her, him, or whatever she is?"

"Safer than if she would have left with any of them sorry ass niggas at Jake's! I been knowing Bea since I was fifteen. One day, I got into a fight with a group of guys and they was beating me real bad. Out of nowhere, Bea came and helped me out. She even pulled a blade and cut one of the boys. She did six months in a home for bad kids for cutting that boy. She didn't even know me but she knew my older brother so she helped me. Once she did her time and got out, we've been close ever since. I know that she has my back more than any of these niggas in the street. Bea Williams is good people and your sister is in good hands!"

I felt a little better but I couldn't stop thinking about it. Cathy was married to Paulie and she up here cheating and got the nerve to be cheating with a woman! But something told me that ain't Cathy first time with no woman.

I got up early the next morning to go to church but all morning it was bothering me that my sister is that kind of woman. I was asking myself what happened to her that made her that way and why she didn't care about what people thought? I prayed harder than I had ever prayed before that God would take that feeling from her cause I know it would kill my Momma to know that her daughter was one of them kind of women.

After church, I couldn't wait to get home. I knew that all my sisters would be there because we planned to have Sunday dinner together at the house. When I got there,

Betty, Burt, and their baby boy, Freddie, Jr., Ernestine, Jeff, Lil Cicely, Butchie Boy, Mally and her boyfriend, Gladys and Cicely was all there. I asked if anybody seen or heard from Cathy and they all said, "No."

"Well y'all know she left with James' funny friend that like women?" They all looked shocked. I went on, "Yeah, Cathy told me that she likes men and women and then she left and went home with Bea."

Cicely said, "When Bea came in last night, Jake told me that she is the biggest number runner in Philly and that she and James is partners and have been for years. He told me that she is one of the meanest and toughest ladies that he ever heard of and that she stabbed a man to death over $50 and ain't nobody say nuthin to the police cause they was too scared!"

"Well I can believe it cause James said that's how they met. He was in a fight when he was fifteen and she helped him out and cut a boy for him and even had to go to a bad kids home for it. They been friends for years."

Ernestine said, "I ain't never knew that girl to be wit no women back home. If Momma knew it'd kill her dead!"

Betty said, "We have to make sure Momma Rosie doesn't find out."

Cicely said, "So what they do bump and eat pu**ys all night? That don't seem like no fun!"

We must have laughed a good ten minutes so we didn't even notice that James, Cathy, and Bea had come

in.

Cathy asked, "What y'all laughin at?" We was all shocked that she was there. Finally, Cicely spoke.

"You and Bea bumpin and eatin pu**y all night!" We all fell out laughing again!

Cathy said, "Y'all wenches is crazy."

Bea said, "Don't knock it til you tried it!" She stuck her tongue out and moved it back and forth real fast. We all laughed even more!

All of the women, except Bea, went into the kitchen and started cooking dinner. We was having a good time, catching up talking about all the folks in the country and all these new folks that we had met up in Philly. It was good to be with my sisters. We were all trying to make better lives for ourselves and our family. Ernestine told us that she had found this home up in Germantown called the Robert Wood Home and that it was a place for working families that needed help with they children while the parents went to work. The kids stayed there all week and went to school out there and they came home on the weekends and that she was letting Lil Cicely and Butchie Boy stay in that home during the week. I asked her if she had been out there to check it out. She said her and Jeff was going out there this week to see about it. Cicely and me told her that we wanted to go see it too.

Once dinner was ready, we were about to sit down when Ernestine asked where was lil Cicely.

Butchie Boy said, "Jeff took her to the store." About

five minutes had passed and they came back and we all sat down to have Sunday dinner.

When my family got together, it was always LOUD! We had so much fun just talking and laughing, it was about 9:00 p.m. when everybody started leaving. Folks had work in the morning.

Cathy stayed with Bea the whole week that she was in Philly. They was getting serious in this short amount of time. When Saturday came and it was time for Cathy to catch her bus, she looked so lovesick to have to be going back to the country to Paulie Saunders. Even though Paulie was a good man and a good father, he didn't give her that spark like Bea.

Before she got on the bus, she whispered in my ear, "I'll be back in a month and me and Bea gonna be togetha. I'm bringin Denise and Lolo and we gonna get a place."

I looked at her and I knew she was serious. I also knew that with Cathy coming to Philly that we really had to get our children and our Momma from down in the country too.

CHAPTER 25

It's Time To Get My Children

SINCE BETTY WAS OUT ON MATERNITY LEAVE, I HAD TO open the office every morning. Mr. Silverstein had started coming in a little later because he was caring for his wife. When he finally came in later that day, I told him that I had to start getting ready to bring my children and Momma up from the country in the next month or so. He offered to help me. He said the first thing I needed to do was get myself a house.

"A house? Mr. Silverstein we talked about this. You know how much you pay me and I can't afford a house."

"Clara, I told you a long time ago that I liked you and that I was going to help you and there are no strings attached. I'm going to give you the money that you need as a down payment and it will be enough to make your mortgage payments affordable!" I didn't know what to say. Before I knew it, I had grabbed him by his neck and was hugging him!

For the first time, I saw Mr. Silverstein in a different way. We were looking into each other's eyes and then we started kissing. He felt all over my body and I liked it.

Before I knew it, he had taken off my dress. He kissed me all over my body and sucked on my breast. I couldn't believe that he knew what he was doing. When he got down to my pu**y, he licked it all over. He sucked it so much that his whole face was covered with my juice. Then, he put his tongue in my hole and no man had ever done that! My pu**y had never been this wet. He turned me over and kissed me up and down my back. He even sucked my toes and kissed all up and down my calves and my thighs. He pulled down his pants and Mr. Silverstein put himself inside of me. He was so gentle and loving and he kissed and held me tight every time he pumped in me. I spread my legs wider cause I wanted all of him inside of me. Mr. Silverstein really knew how to make love and not just thrusting his d**k in me. I had never, in all my years of having relations, felt like this. He loved me and it was real love. Once we finished, I think we were both a little embarrassed. We didn't expect nothing like that to happen, I know I sure didn't.

"Clara, in all my years of making love to a woman, I have never felt like I just felt when I was with you."

"Mr. Siverstein, I have to be honest too. I have never felt that way either being with a man." He smiled and looked relieved. Then I said, "But you have a wife and I have a boyfriend and this isn't right."

"Let's not think about them and just focus on us and this moment!" He pulled the blinds shut and put the closed sign on the door and Mr. Silverstein and me made

beautiful love all day long.

Well, that was until the phone rang. We had fell asleep and had been ignoring the phone all day. I told him that I better answer it cause it was 4:00 p.m. When I picked up, it was Mrs. Silverstein.

"Hello, Clara? I've been calling there all day and the phone has been just ringing off the hook. Is everything all right?"

At that moment, I really felt bad for what I had done. Here this lady is home sick with cancer and I'm f**kin her husband.

"Clara? Can you hear me? Clara?"

"Yes, ma'am, I can hear you. We had trouble with the phone lines all day. The man from the phone company just left here and got it working again. Would you like to speak to Mr. Silverstein?"

"Oh, good, I was worried that something had happened! Okay yes, please put my husband on."

"Okay, please hold for a minute," I said.

Before I could hit the hold button, she said, "And Clara, have a nice day!"

I felt like sh*t! Here she was telling me to have a nice day and I just did you know what, with her husband while she has cancer! And on top of that, I'm a liar too.

"You have a nice day too."

The look on Mr. Silverstein's face showed that reality had just set in for him too. I left out so he could take the call. I heard him pick up and say, "Yes Dear, yes something

happened to the phone line and..."

I closed his office door because I didn't want to hear what they were talking about. I had to get myself cleaned up and together before James picked me up. I didn't want him getting wind of what had just happened between me and Mr. Silverstein but I knew I was floating on air. I knew things would never be the same between James and me ever again. I had fallen in love with Mr. Silverstein. This was too much for one afternoon.

When I got in the car with James, I acted like I wasn't feeling well. I asked him to take me home because I had a bad stomach ache and needed to get to my bed. He didn't ask any questions and drove me right home. Before he dropped me off, he asked if I needed anything and I told him that I just wanted to rest. I kissed him on the cheek and went in the house. All night, I tossed and turned thinking about what had happened between Mr. Silverstein and me. I couldn't tell anybody because they would think I was crazy cause I thought I was crazy.

The next day when I got to work, I was still a little bashful but Mr. Silverstein made me feel okay. He had a paper that had all of the homes for sale in West Philly, not the bottom of West Philly either, but on Cedar Avenue and Pine Street, where white folks lived. I was so excited he said that we were going to start closing the office for lunch and checking out some of these homes. Things were lining up for me to get my children and my Momma out of the country.

I told Mr. Silvestein about the Robert Wood Home and he thought it was a good idea since I would still be able to work during the week and spend time with the kids on the weekends. I made plans to go with Ernestine, Jeff, and Cicely to see the place.

When we got there, the house was one of those big old homes in Germantown with a wraparound porch and a big sign out front that said, ROBERT WOOD HOME FOR CHILDREN. A nice, older couple ran the home and their two teenaged children also lived there and helped out. We saw the entire house, including the kid's room, kitchen, and play area. They even took us around the corner to see the elementary school and junior high school where the children would be attending. It would be good for them, especially since they would all be together. We decided that we'd take turns picking them up on the weekends. We agreed to start the children there in one month.

I was happy that we found a place for the children to stay during the week, now I needed a place that they could be on the weekends and somewhere that Momma would be happy too. Mr. Silverstein and me were going out everyday at lunch looking at places.

One day he said, "Let's check out this place on 49th and Cedar Avenue. It's a two-family home."

"What's a two-family home?"

"It's when you have one house with two separate entrances."

"That sounds so nice!"

Later that day, we went to see it and I fell in love! I told him it was the house I wanted.

He said, "Then this is the house you will get!"

He took care of everything and put the house in my name. He told me that I would be responsible for paying the mortgage but it was so low that I could pay it out of one paycheck. He told me if I doubled my payments every month, the house would be paid off in fifteen years rather than thirty. Mr. Silverstein had taught me so much and given me so much, I was truly grateful to him.

What am I going to tell James and my sisters? That I just up and bought a house? I hadn't mentioned it to anybody and I just went about my business and did it? Things had been a little funny between me and James anyway since I slept with Mr. Silverstein so I know this wasn't gonna sit well with him. One thing was for sure, I was moving in and then figuring out a way to go get Momma and my children.

Once everything was settled and I had the keys, I wanted to bring my sisters to the house. Mr. Silverstein made sure that I had nice furniture and that the kids and Momma had a nice bed to sleep on. The plan was to rent the other side out so that I could double up on the mortgage payments to pay the house off quicker but I wasn't sure cause I wanted to have my own space for once.

I told my sister's that I had a surprise to show them and that I needed them to meet me at 4907 Cedar Avenue

on Tuesday at 5:30p.m. sharp. They all wanted to know what the big surprise was down there. I was able to hold it, though it was killing me and I made sure to tell them not to say nothing about the surprise in front of James.

When Tuesday came, I could hardly focus at work. Mr. Silverstein knew that I was showing my sisters the house so he let me leave at 4:00p.m. to go run any last-minute errands. I could hardly believe that I owned a house—a nice house in a nice neighborhood. My Momma was finally gonna get off that ole farm. I went to the store and picked up something to drink and a few things that we could nibble on while we were in my new house. I like the way that sounded, my new house. It was all mine!

When my sisters got to the house, they rang the doorbell. I opened the door smiling and they stood looking at me like I was crazy.

Betty said, "Clara, whose house is this, and why are you answering their door?"

I said, "Mine and this is my door!"

They looked at me like I was crazy. Of course, Cicely was first to say something.

"Girl, stop playin wit us and tell us who house this is before the owner come home and throw your tail in jail!"

"No, really! This is my house. Both the bottom and top floor. Y'all come on in and look around!"

I opened the screen door and let them in. Once they came in and looked around, they started believing more and more that it really was my house. I had been bringing

a few items over here and there, but I didn't want to bring too much cause I still hadn't told James and them either up until this point. They were so happy for me. I told them my plans to bring Momma and my children up and even told Cicely that Benji could come and stay with me until she figured out something. We were all so happy and couldn't wait to get our family out of the country. Then Ernestine said, "You know Momma ain't gonna leave the country witout Walter and Carrie!"

I hadn't even thought about them cause they was grown as far as I was concerned.

We sat for awhile talking and I explained how Mr. Silverstein had helped me get the house. I was telling them all that he had taught Betty and me and one of them said, "Well, what did you teach him?"

They all laughed and I turned red.

"Don't worry about that! Whatever I taught him was enough to get me this house!" We all laughed until tears came down our faces.

Ernestine said she got a letter from Cathy saying that she and the children would be up here in two weeks and that she was leaving Paulie for good.

"That damn Bea done put something on that one. She left her husband and everything," I said.

Ernestine said, "You one to talk! You done left James' Black ass for your white boss!" We hollered cause she was right.

It was getting late, so Ernestine said she had to go.

I asked her where the children was and she said that Butchie Boy went to the neighbors' house after school and that Jeff usually picked up lil Cicely and would take her around with him places. Jeff seemed real good with the kids, especially Lil Cicely. She was always with him and he was always buying her toys and candy, pretty much whatever she wanted. Ernestine was lucky to have someone in her corner helping out with them especially since she worked the night shift at Horn & Harderts. Sometimes to make a little extra cash, she would still help Cicely down at Jake's. Jeff worked in the day, so he would be home with the kids at night while she worked. Things was lining up for the Fortune girls just like we planned.

CHAPTER 26

All The Children Is Moving To Philly

I STAYED WITH JAMES LONG ENOUGH TO GET HIM TO TAKE ME back down to the country to get my children. That was two of the hardest things I ever had to do, pretend to like him and take those children from my Momma! Nobody seemed like they were happy that they were leaving except for Carrie.

"You shoulda been done came and got them. Leaving all these chilren here for me and Momma to raise," she yelled. "Take them on up to Philly with you and learn how to be a Momma for once in your life! Now you got your own house, you can really see what it's like raisin chilren!"

James looked at me strangely when Carrie mentioned me owning my own house. I still hadn't told him. He didn't say nothing right then cause I'm sure he didn't know if I had just lied to them but he didn't look happy either way. I had told Momma in the letter I wrote her when I told her about coming to get the children.

Neither Benji nor Elleeboo was happy about coming

to Philly and Juanita was downright mad. She didn't understand why she had to leave, she wasn't the one giving Momma problems and she did not want to live in Philly. I tried to tell them all the good things about it but all they knew was the country and that's where they wanted to be. I told them Momma was gonna come to Philly within the next year but they wanted to wait and come when she came. I told them we had to get things ready for her.

None of them cared nothing about what I was saying and when it was time to leave, they all acted a fool. Momma was crying, they was all crying, and Carrie was sitting in a corner laughing like the devil. Walter May was hung over as usual and fussing and carrying on because everybody was hollering and crying and he couldn't sleep. It broke my heart to leave Momma there with Carrie and Walter May but I knew that she wouldn't be able to stay away from her grand children for no length of time.

On the drive back, once the children fell asleep, James said, "What's this talk about you owning your own house? Was that what you had to tell your Momma in order for her to feel safe with you bringing your children to Philly?"

I was quiet for a minute, and I said, "That's what I told her and it's also true. I bought a little house in West Philly."

He looked at me and said, "You bought a house and you didn't bother to tell me nothing about it?"

I said, in a real sassy way, "Some things are better that you don't know!" Folks don't like when you give them they own medicine.

"What did you say?"

I thought about it and realized I didn't want me and the children to get put out on the side of the road, so I said, "Well, I didn't really know how to tell you because Mr. Silverstein was helping me out and getting all of the information for me."

"Mr. Silverstein, your boss? Now why in the world is he helping you get a house?"

"Because he knew I needed to have a place for my children and Momma to come to. I don't know nobody else that care enough to think about that."

"Clara you never asked me to help."

"I never asked Mr. Silverstein eitha. He offered."

He got real quiet and we didn't speak for about five minutes and then he said, "This explains why you've been so cold to me lately."

I didn't say a word and we were quiet the rest of the way back to Philly. When we reached Philly, he asked, "Are you going to your new house?"

"No, you can drop us by Gladys'!" When he got in front of Gladys' house, he took the bags out the trunk and didn't even say bye. He just drove off.

That wasn't the way I wanted things to end with James, but it wasn't right to hold on to him knowing I didn't feel the same about him anymore.

The kids still weren't happy to be in Philly but they were happy that they were all together again. When Butchie Boy and Cicely saw Juanita, Elleeboo, and Benji, they lit up like it was Christmas. They started hugging and then they asked if they could go outside. They had a lot of catching up to do. All of them were staying at my house until it was time for them to go to the Robert Wood Home. They had two weeks before school started and we had a lot to do to get everybody ready. They needed clothes, shoes, and school supplies.

Jake had given me money to make sure that everybody got what they needed especially since they were all staying with me. Shucks, I was the only one that had enough space for everybody. Ernestine and Jeff did go out and buy food and brought it over, but Jeff didn't seem too happy about lil Cicely staying with me for two weeks. He thought she should be spending more time at home since they were going be staying up at the Robert Wood Home. He didn't have a problem with Butchie Boy staying, but he was real protective over lil Cicely. Ernestine put her foot down and said she was staying with her brother and cousins and that was it.

For the next week, all we did was shop, eat, and go to different places in the city so the children wouldn't be so homesick and keep asking for Momma. They were starting to lighten up, even Juanita was laughing and smiling. Everybody was behaving and not being so mean and sassy. Juanita had been calling me Clara since

she could talk and always called my Momma, Momma. One day we were all in Fairmount Park and there was some type of fair with all kinds of stands where people were selling art, jewelry, food and a whole lot of other stuff. Juanita was so excited when she saw a table where a woman was selling pretty bands that went around your hair.

She yelled, "Momma! Come over here! Can I have one of these bands?"

It threw me off cause this was the first time she ever called me Momma and the first time she ever asked me for anything. I didn't let her know that it threw me off. I acted normal and bought her three of the bands. I was sure hoping that this would be the start of us having a better relationship.

Juanita had grown to be a beautiful young girl. She had beautiful hair, skin, and body like a brick sh*thouse. That's what the men in Hustle would say when a lady had a nice shape. I loved Juanita so much and knew I had missed a lot of time with her growing up so I was trying to make up for lost time. But I didn't know how she was going to feel when they found out they had to stay at the Robert Wood Home. We still didn't tell them because we didn't want to upset them more than they already were. We would find out soon cause we all had to work and these children needed to be looked after. That week, Mr. Silverstein let me get off early while we got them settled. They would turn the house upside down if nobody was

home to watch over them all day.

A week and a half had gone by and we made plans to take the children out to lunch. That's when we were going to take them to see the Robert Wood Home and where they were going to go to school. They were excited to be going out to lunch. They were all talking about what they were going to eat, and asking if they could get ice cream? What they didn't know is that Cathy was back in Philly with Denise and Lolo and they were all meeting us for lunch. They were going to be staying at the Robert Wood Home too. Bea was paying for them to stay because she had an apartment that wasn't too far from there but it wasn't large enough for the kids.

When we got to the restaurant and the kids saw each other, they ran to one another and hugged and jumped up and down. You would've thought that they hadn't seen each other in years. But I guess they felt comfortable around each other because Philly was much different than Hustle.

At lunch, the children had hamburgers for the first time and couldn't get enough of them. The one thing they liked about being in Philly was all the different foods they could try. Down in the country, they didn't have a lot of choices. They ate everything on the hog, the cow, the chicken, and a lot of potatoes. Up here, there was Italians that made fresh pasta and hoagies. Then you had the Polish people that sold hotdogs and sausages with peppers and onions that made you wanna slap your momma! We

wanted the children to learn new things so we made sure they tried all of those foods and they loved them all.

Once lunch was finished, we let them get ice cream. They were extra excited about that. While they were eating their ice cream, we decided it was time to tell them about the Robert Wood Home. We agreed that Ernestine would be the one to do most of the talking since she found the place and we would help her out if she needed it. Besides, the children didn't talk back too much to Ernestine because she was no nonsense and would knock your head off.

She stood up and put her hand on her hip and patted her foot. She always did that when she was nervous or serious.

"We hope that y'all is liking it here in Philly. We knows that y'all miss Momma and being in the country, but Momma is gettin old and y'all chilren was down there actin up and made it hard on her. So we all been workin to get y'all up here and now we is real happy that y'all is here.

Now that y'all is here, y'all gots to do real good in school. That's going to help you make somethin of yourselves. And since we all work," she was pointing at all the sisters, "we had to find a place for all y'all to stay during the week." Then she pointed at all of them. Then she said, "Y'all are gonna stay at a real nice place called the Robert Wood Home and we gonna come get y'all on the weekends."

First, it was quiet for about two minutes then Benji said, "So y'all done brought us up to Philly and took us from Momma for us to live wit somebody else? I wanna go back and stay on the farm!" He looked at Cicely like he wanted to kill her.

Elleeboo said, "My Momma on the farm anyway! I never wanted to come up here!" And put his head down. Denise and Lolo hollered and cried because they'd never lived away from their Momma and Poppa. Lolo asked Cathy, "Who is we gonna live wit? Why can't we live wit you?"

Cathy said, "Lolo, I have to find work and who gonna be home wit y'all after school?"

Denise said, "I want to go back wit my Poppa!"

Butchie Boy and lil Cicely were crying too as everybody in the restaurant was staring at us. Juanita looked at me like I was the devil himself! She rolled her eyes at me while trying to keep the little ones from crying.

I heard her whisper to lil Cicely, "They don't want us around cause they old boyfriends probably don't like chilren, but I'mma take care of us!"

I could have sworn I heard lil Cicely whisper back, "No, Mr. Jeff like me. He always kissin me and touching my bookie!"

Juanita said, "What you say girl?"

She saw that I was looking and nudged lil Cicely and gave her a look that told her to hush. Lil Cicely looked around like she was scared to death and sunk down in the

seat and covered her face and started crying even more.

Touch her bookie? Bookie is what we called our pu**y when we were little girls and it was passed down to all of us. My momma called it a bookie and my aunties called it a bookie too. It was passed down to all my sisters and we taught our chilren that it was a bookie. It's not until you get older that you learn the real name is a pu**y. But did she say that Jeff was touching her bookie?

CHAPTER 27

Remembering Old Times

ALL DAY I COULDN'T GET IT OFF MY MIND. IT WAS bothering me so bad about what I thought I heard that child say, but I wasn't sure and I couldn't go starting no mess if I wasn't sure. When we reached the Robert Wood Home, the kids were acting kind of shy. We knew they would like the house because it was big and beautiful. There were two sides, one for the boys and one for the girls and they shared the play areas. Once they saw the bedroom and the bathrooms, and they knew that they were all going to be together and sharing rooms, they seemed to be okay. After what I thought I heard lil Cicely say, I was even more for the chilren being up here. At least she'd be away from Jeff while Ernestine was at work. We told Mr. and Mrs. Wood that all of the children would be moving in on that Monday and that we would have them all set up for school.

Before we went back to my house, we stopped by the children's new schools. The elementary school, where the little ones were going, was right across the street from the junior high school, where the bigger kids were going.

Cathy told the older ones, "Y'all is to drop off the lil chilren in the morning and you is to pick them up once school is over. If anything happens to one of these lil ones, y'all older ones is gonna get the sh*t beat out of you. Y'all here? And y'all lil ones, you better listen to every word they say or y'all assess gonna get whooped too!"

They all said, "Yes ma'am!"

My mind hadn't been right since we were in the restaurant. How am I going to find out if Jeff is touching this girl? This thing happened all the time in the country, but the only thing is, don't nobody care much. But I know how it felt to have some grown ass man touching on you, especially when it's your own kinfolk. I was 11 years old, a little older than lil Cicely, when it happened to me. Momma had sent me to cousin Matilda's house for some butter. Cousin Matilda lived about a mile up the road from us so I was playing and skipping along, having a good ole time by myself. I seen Ms. Dolly on the way, she was one of Momma's friends from church. She asked me where I was heading and I told her to get some butter from cousin Matilda's. She gave me one of those butterscotch candies that were wrapped in the gold paper. I was happy I was by myself cause if somebody was with me, I'd have to bite it into pieces so everybody could get a taste. That's how we were raised. You had to share with your siblings. I sucked it slow so it would last, that butterscotch tasted so good!

When I got there, I knocked on the door and cousin Matilda's husband, cousin Dave, came to the door. I said, "Hi cousin Dave, is cousin Matilda here? My Momma sent me here to get some butter."

He started looking at me real funny and rubbing on his chest. He opened the door wide and said, "Come on in here gal."

Once I got in he closed the door behind him. I was standing there looking around to see where everybody was.

He said, "Your cousin Matilda ain't home right now but she'll be back in a minute so sit down and wait for her."

He pointed over to where the chair was so I went and sat on the chair. He came over and said, "Get on up from that chair, that's my chair."

I stood up and was about to go to the other chair and then he sat down in his chair and grabbed my arm and was pulling me to him. I was trying to pull away and then he grabbed me hard and said, "Come on over here and sit on cousin Dave's lap."

I knew I wasn't supposed to sit on grown men's laps so I tried to pull away again and said, "I can sit on the other chair!"

He grabbed and pulled me back and said, "No, it's okay. I want you to sit over here wit me!"

When he sat me on his lap, I could feel his man parts on my butt. It was big and hard like a tree branch and he

was rubbing it back and forth on my butt. I was so scared that I swallowed my candy, but I was too scared to move.

I felt like I was choking on the candy! He started going up my dress and touching my bookie and rubbing it and then he took one of his fingers and jammed it in my hole. It hurt so bad. He was kissing all over me and touching on me and his breath smelled like whiskey. I still couldn't move and didn't say a word. I was just hoping he'd stop.

"Clara, I had my eye on you for awhile. You is gonna be one mighty fine woman." He was pumping on my butt and had his finger up inside me.

Then he took me in the bedroom where he and cousin Matilda sleep and took off all my clothes. He made me put his man parts in my mouth and he told me to lick all over it like it was a sucker and he did the same to my bookie. He was sucking all on my nipples and rubbing his man parts all over me. I knew this was wrong and he wasn't supposed to be doing this to me but I was too scared to say a word! Then, he pushed his man parts in my bookie. He was pushing and pushing and it wouldn't fit. It was hurting so bad, each time he pushed harder and kept telling me to open my legs up. He was holding my legs up with his arms and it still wouldn't fit.

He got up and got some petroleum from off the dresser and rubbed it all over my bookie. He put his finger in me again and was kissing all over me. Then he pushed and pushed it in me again and it was hurting so bad. All

of a sudden, it was like a pop and I screamed so loud! I was in so much pain it felt like someone had stabbed me in my bookie with a knife.

"Hush up gal for somebody hear you!"

I was squirming and still screaming and he took his hand and covered my mouth and told me, "Shut up for I slap you!" He was moving his thang all around inside me and pounding on me so hard that after a while my bookie was just swollen and numb. He just kept saying how good and sweet this pu**y was. I didn't know what was happening. He turned me every which way. Made me get on my knees like I was a dog. He sat me on top of him. It seemed like this went on for hours. He'd said cousin Matilda would be right back. I was wondering, where was she.

When he finished his business, he pulled his thang out of me and all this white stuff came out. I ain't know what that was, but he said, "That right there is so you don't come up wit no chile!"

Then he threw my dress to me. He looked down at the bed and it was all this blood on his yellow sheets and I looked down at my bookie and it was bleeding, red and swollen too. I could barely walk to pick up my dress.

"Damn it! What I'mma tell Madeline happened to this bed?" He started walking back and forth rubbing his head, and then I guess he came up with something. He whispered under his breath, "I'mma tell her I had a nose bleed!" Then he started pulling the sheets off the bed and

he looked over at me. I was putting my dress back on. He got this real mean look in his eyes and said, "I swear if you tell one soul about what just happened..."

He went and grabbed his rifle and put it right on my temple. "I will kill you!"

Pee ran down my leg as I stood there shaking and bleeding.

"Yes, sir."

Then he pointed to the door with his rifle and said, "Now, get on up the road!"

I ran outta that house so fast, I forgot all about the pain. When I made it back to the farm, I had to be looking and smelling a mess.

Momma came on the porch and said, "Gal, what's chasin you?"

"Huh?"

"You come running down that road like something was after you and why is blood running down your leg?"

"Huh?"

I looked down at the blood that was running down my leg from my bookie.

She yelled, "Gal, what done got into you? Is you crazy? Why is you bleeding?"

I wanted to yell "COUSIN DAVE MAN PARTS DONE GOT IN ME, THAT'S WHAT!" But I kept thinking about that rifle pointed at my head so I said, "I was running and fell on a rock and skinned my thigh."

"Come here let me clean it up."

I told her that cousin Matilda had already cleaned it up and put something on it.

"Well get a rag and clean up all that dry blood for the mosqitas and flies eat you up!"

"Yes ma'am!"

Then she asked for the butter.

"She ain't have none."

I didn't think I was ever going to be able to sit down again. My bookie was raw and bloody and it was hurting so bad. I tried to stay from around Momma and my sisters until I was feeling better cause I was so light that my thighs were all bruised up. I know they would have asked me all kind of questions so I never told a soul.

I was off in my own head thinking about what cousin Dave had done to me that I didn't hear them calling me to leave. Ernestine came over and shook me and said, "Clara what's wrong wit you girl? You don't hear us talkin to you?"

"I'm sorry. I was just deep in my thoughts!"

Rolling her eyes she said, "Well come on, we leavin."

Four months had passed and the children were getting used to being at the Robert Wood Home. The boys were always still in some kind of trouble and the rules at the Home were that if you act up during the week, you couldn't come home on the weekends, instead you'd have to stay there and do chores. The boys hadn't been

home in a month. We would see them when we picked up lil Cicely and Denise every other weekend. Juanita didn't come home either when the boys were in trouble, she'd rather stay up there with them than to come home with me. Deep down, she was mad that I left and came to Philly and now she was also mad because she was living there.

Every other Friday, Jeff would be waiting at my house for one of us to bring the girls back. If he wasn't waiting out front when we got there, it wasn't five minutes before we got in the door that he was ringing the bell to pick up lil Cicely. Lil Cicely was growing up to be a pretty chocolate thang with pretty thick black hair and big light brown eyes. She was a bit of a tomboy. She was cute and sweet as a button, but she was always in trouble for fighting.

One Friday, Jeff picked her up and said, "Ernestine said to tell you that she got a letter from your Momma. She wants to leave the farm for good before Christmas. Carrie moved in with Robbie Reynolds so your Momma and Walter May is coming to Philly!"

I was thinking to myself, I'll take in my Momma, but nobody said anything about Walter's drunk, spoiled ass! I know Momma wasn't going to leave the country without him, so he had to come too.

I thought in my mind that I was ready for my Momma to come, but was I? It's going to be okay, they can just stay upstairs on the other side of the house and I

won't rent it out. I know one thing, Walter May is going to have to get a job, stop all that drinking, and help out with the bills.

Christmas was one week away. Me and Ernestine went down to meet Walter May and Momma at the bus. We were both shocked when we saw Walter May. He looked good! He had stopped all the drinking and hanging out. Momma said she told him if he didn't stop drinking and carrying on, she was moving to Philly and leaving him down in Hustle. Momma said he hadn't had a drink in five months. I was proud of my baby brother. He said he was ready to clean himself up and get his life in order with God and that he would be going to church with me. He promised to get a job and help out with Momma, the children, and bills.

"Okay, slow down and take a breath. I hear you," I said. "Let's get you all settled in then we can start planning." In my mind, it all sounded good but I wanted to see how things worked out. But I liked what he was saying. Our family needed a good man leading it.

The kids were coming home for Christmas so we surprised them when they got to the house, Momma and Walter May were there. They were happy they were staying at the house with Momma for Christmas break. Christmas had to be the best ever. The kids got everything they'd asked for, but best of all, our whole family was

together except for Carrie. This was my dream since the day that I got on that Greyhound to come to Philly!

After Christmas break, the kids went back to the Home, but the boys stopped getting in trouble so they could come home on the weekends and stay with Momma. We were able to keep lil Cicely away from Jeff cause no way Jeff was going to argue with Momma! Walter May went to church every Sunday and even got a job at a warehouse driving a forklift. He did exactly what he planned. He was getting himself together.

CHAPTER 28

*Sh*t Is Getting Bad*

I T'S BEEN ALMOST SIX MONTHS SINCE ME AND JAMES BROKE up and I missed him. James was the manly type that took care of his woman. I always had a ride and we'd do things together. Plus, he was always good to my family. Momma always said, "You never miss your water til your well runs dry." Now I know what that meant. I didn't have Mr. Silverstein to lean on because he was spending more time at home and away from the office cause his wife's cancer was getting worse. She needed a lot of care. I was really running the office because he was never there. But this was the least I could do for him after all he had done for me. I felt bad for them because their life had changed so much. He didn't do nothing but take care of her and take her to doctor appointments. It was wearing on him too. His hair used to be salt and pepper but now it was just salt and he looked old and tired.

I would see James every now and then at Jake's and he would act like he never knew me. He'd talk to all of my sisters but never me. Cathy would fill me in on how he was doing cause him and Bea was still close and working

together. She said he wasn't seeing anybody and that he was drinking a lot and had been getting sloppy with the business. I was shocked cause this didn't sound like the James I knew. She said Bea said he took our break up real hard cause he trusted me and that I betrayed him and bought a house with my white boss. She said he told Bea that he had been saving up to buy us a house in Williamstown, New Jersey and he was gonna ask me to marry him. She said he was messed up because he never loved a woman the way he did me and that he hadn't been right ever since. I told Cathy that I didn't want to hear anymore. Me and James were in the past and I did what I needed to do for our family.

Cathy said, "No, you did what you had to do for you." They never did understand that every move I made was for my family.

Jake's lounge was finally on the map! After four years of having the best food, drinks, bands, and the baddest woman running the place, people were now coming from other states on the weekends to hang at Jake's. Cicely had come in and stepped the place up. We never talked about it, but word was that Cicely had call girls in the club now and that she made a lot of money off them. I knew all those women because they called her Sugie. Cicely had learned a lot from Jake and one thing she didn't do is talk about their business with us. She gave us all nice things but we knew not to ask questions. All the big-time men came to Jake's too. They had their fancy cars, clothes,

jewelry, and always smelled good. Whenever they called her Sugie, I knew they were the men coming in for those women. She even had white men that loved colored girls and they would come looking for Sugie's girls.

Jake's Lounge was rolling! All summer the place was packed every week from Wednesday to Sunday. People loved to go there. Other local clubs were closing down because they couldn't compete with the crowds that Jake's was pulling in. The colored bar and restaurant owners were not happy that this white Mafia man was able to come into their neighborhood and take all of the colored people away from their colored-owned businesses. They would threaten Jake and threaten to burn down the place. They hated Cicely even more because she was a colored woman. They would say stuff like, "He using you to tear down your own neighborhood! You ain't nothing but a hoe to him!"

Cicely didn't give a damn as long as she could take care of her family. She'd do rude stuff to them, like turn up her ass and tell them to kiss it or give them the middle finger.

One day, we were getting out the car at Shapiro's and Warren Baker came up to us. He owned the Touch of Class Bar on Haverford Avenue, maybe three or four blocks from Jake's. He was an ugly, black nigga with craters all in his face and had the nerve to have a missing tooth in the front of his mouth. He had a process in his hair and wore bright ass polyester suits. He was from North

Caroline and they said he was a pimp too. He usually had some straggly little woman with him but today, he was by himself. He walked over to us.

"If it ain't Jake the Snake's little mistress," He said rubbing his ugly ass chin. "I heard about you but I ain't never seen you this close up." He walked around us looking us up and down. "You is a nice, fine, piece of ass!" He came closer which gave me an even clearer look at just how ugly he was.

Me and Cicely just stood there.

"So how much would it cost to get two hoes like you to come work for me?"

I could sense Cicely getting angry. She smirked, put her hand on her hip, and walked over to him before getting right up in his face.

In a sugary sweet voice, she said, "First, it would take you choppin your ugly f**kin head off cause I couldn't stomach to look at your black monkey face. Oh, and then you'd have to have a bunch of money like this..." She pulled out a wad of money that she had rolled up in her bra and threw it in his face! She turned around to walk off, leaving him looking like a raging bull.

He lifted up his hand and it was like I saw it in slow motion. I screamed, "Cicely! Watch ou-" and before I could finish the warning, his hand came down and he had slapped her on the side of her face and head.

"Don't no two-bit whore talk to me like that. Is you crazy bi*ch?"

I saw the devil when he entered Cicely and before I could get over to her, she'd pulled a blade out of her breast. When she turned around, she swung the knife and cut him right in his face! Blood gushed out everywhere! He grabbed his face and yelled, "This crazy bi*ch cut me!" She sliced him to the white meat!

He ran backwards trying to get into his car but Cicely was still heading towards him. I grabbed her arm.

"Cicely! Stop!" She tried to get at him but I was holding her back.

"This ugly Black motherf**ka think he gonna hit me! I'll kill his Black ass!" I pushed her to get in the car so we could leave because people were starting to gather around.

When we left, she made me promise not to tell nobody because Jake was already worried about her and wanted her to slow down and start thinking about maybe having some babies. She didn't want no parts of that and if he knew about this, she was sure he'd make her stay away from Jake's and she had big plans. I promised her that I wouldn't tell the bushes. That was another one of Momma's sayings. Do not tell the bushes if you don't want nobody to know, cause if the wind blow, they might tell.

"What makes you think Warren isn't gonna say nothing?"

"Cause he'd die before he let it get out that a woman cut him!"

CHAPTER 29

It's Time To Grow

CICELY LAID LOW FOR A COUPLE OF WEEKS TO FEEL things out. While she was out, she came up with some great ideas on ways to make Jake's even bigger. She had extra time to think about how she can piss Warren and the rest of the niggas off that didn't like how she and Jake were growing their business.

Jake's was going to be like one of those fancy places in center city where the white folks hung out but with the same soul food, drinks, and bands as before. People were gonna love it. It was all Cicely talked about. Every time we were around her, she was asking us about paint or curtains or glasses, always something to do with the new place.

A month had gone by and Cicely was starting to relax a little more. They had worked out all of the paperwork to get the new place and she hadn't heard nothing from Warren. They were closing down for two months while all the work was being done. Cicely and Jake planned a big party the night before the temporary closing. They hired a band all the way from New York. They had the hottest

record out called, "My Baby is Back." People were talking about this night for a couple of weeks. It was going to be a big crowd. Cicely took all of us, even Walter, out to get stuff to wear to the big party.

When the night of the party came, we were all casket sharp. That's what the old people back home said when you were clean. We had all gotten our hair done and all of the sisters were coming out. Everybody was ready and excited. It was one of those perfect September nights. The weather was mild and it was a full moon so the city was bright. You know what they say about a full moon, that's when the crazy stuff happens. There was a natural buzz in the air that this was going to be a night to remember.

When we got to the club, the line was already down the street. We'd never seen a crowd this big, but then again, they'd never had a band this big playing at Jake's. Plus, everybody knew that they were closing until New Year's Eve when they planned to open the bigger place. We went straight to the front of the line and Larry let us in. We walked over to our usual section. The band was warming up and sounding good. The lead singer kept looking over at me but I knew James was going to be in there and I was hoping that we would be able to talk. Every time he would look over at me, I looked away.

The place was getting packed. The band was jamming and people were ordering drinks and food left and right. Cicely had so much food and whiskey sent over to our

table that it wasn't room for nothing else. People kept piling in the place and the line was still wrapped around the corner. It didn't look like everybody was going to get in. I had never seen this many people trying to get into one place. I saw James when he came in and he didn't look like himself. He was stumbling like he had already started drinking before he got there. His clothes weren't pressed, his hair wasn't cut, and he didn't look like he'd shaved in a couple of weeks. This was not the James I knew. What was going on with him?

He went over in the corner talking to Bea and some man. Cathy went over to where they were when she saw Bea come in and you could see that whatever Bea said to her, she danced off and went about her business. It was strange to see how Cathy just listened to any and everything Bea told her to do. She never listened to Paulie like that, or anybody for that matter. It looked to me like James was arguing with the man but Bea got in between them and she pushed James away. He looked like he said something to Bea and then he went to the bar and ordered a drink, like his drunk ass needed another drink. Bea stood there for a minute and finished talking to the guy. It looked like she was trying to calm him down. Whatever they were talking about, he must have still been pissed at James because he kept pointing at him. James sure wasn't in any condition to defend himself if things got out of hand. I watched the whole thing.

There were so many people in the lounge that it was

hard to move around. People were bumping into one another, dancing all over the place, and having a good time. This band was so good, they had the spot jumping with every song they played. The ladies were gyrating all over the place and the men were loving it and giving it right back. This was definitely the biggest night that Jake's Lounge had ever had!

I was making my way through the crowd, trying to make my way back to our section when a guy bumped into me, spilling his drink all over me. I wanted to be mad but he was so nice and apologetic and was trying to clean me up.

When I looked up at him, he looked familiar but I couldn't remember how I knew him. He was a nice-looking man with pretty white teeth and a scar over his left eye. He was dressed real nice and he was with a couple of fellas and they were dressed real nice too.

"I'm so sorry Miss!"

I could barely hear him over the music so I said, "Huh?"

He repeated himself and I told him that it was okay. Now we were both trying to clean me up. He asked if he could buy me a drink and I told him that I should be buying him a drink since he spilled his drink all over me. We laughed and I told him that I was fine and making my way back to my table where I had plenty of drinks and food. He apologized again and I gave him a little wave and walked off. As I walked away, I couldn't stop thinking

about where I knew him from. His face was so familiar.

I finally pushed my way back to our section and everybody was dancing to the jam, "Love Gonna Get Ya." The lounge was going crazy. I had my eyes closed and was feeling the song. When I opened my eyes, I saw the man that spilled the drink on me looking at me and he was talking to some guys and pointing over at James. Maybe that's where I knew him from, maybe he knew me from being with James. I still couldn't picture how I knew him. About five minutes went by and it finally hit me where I knew him from. He was the guy that James beat down in the street across from Tootsie's! What was he doing here?

Jake's is the best lounge in Philly and half of Philly was in here. Did he know that James would be here? Are they about to hurt James? He was in there with his friends and James was in no condition to fight if they wanted to start something. I had to warn James that he was in here and get him out of Jake's before anything went down.

I made my way over to the bar and tried to talk to James and before I could say anything, he looked over at me and I knew he was drunk.

"You are dead to me!" He said through slurred words. He looked away and started drinking his drink. I tried to tell him about the man but he cut me off and said, "Bi*ch, you didn't hear what I said! Get the f**k away from me!"

I guess I looked as stupid as I felt because I felt like the whole bar was watching us. I never thought that

James would have that much hatred towards me. It stung so much, I was about to leave the lounge.

Cathy must have seen what happened and came over and said, "Don't waste your time on James, he ain't the same man you knew. Forget about him girl. Let's have us some fun!" She gave me a drink and started dancing and pulling me out onto the dance floor. I downed the drink in one gulp and before I knew it, I was dancing all over the place and had forgot all about James. The singer that was looking at me earlier was singing to me. Now, I really wasn't paying James any mind. I danced for most the night and when I wasn't dancing, I was talking to that fine singer. Ernestine, Mally, and Betty were having fun too. Jeff didn't come out and I saw Ernestine talking to this man that lived across the street from her and Jeff and they looked liked more than neighbors. James was still at the bar and he was drinking and drinking and getting wasted. Jake went over to talk to him but it looked like he pushed Jake away too, like he didn't want to be bothered.

This was the best night that Jake's ever had. I saw those working girls going in and out the place all night, so I know that Sugie made some good money off them. I always laughed my tale off when they called Cicely, Sugie. The bar and the kitchen were rolling too! Cicely had ordered a lot of booze and food cause she knew it was going to be a lot of people coming out.

Right before the lounge was about to close, we heard what sounded like bottles breaking and loud yelling like

there was about to be a fight. The band stopped playing and Cathy and me stood up on our table to see what was happening. We looked towards the bar to see the guy that James had beat up and his friends trying to get at James but Bea was standing in front of him with a broken bottle in her hand and one of the guy's friends on the floor bleeding. She had hit the guy over the head with the bottle and dared the other ones to make a move and she was going to cut their throats! Cathy went running over there but before she could get there, Larry and the other bouncers came and threw the guy and his friends out. They wouldn't throw Bea and James out because they knew they were family. James was still drinking and talking sh*t! After Bea saved his ass from getting beat to death, he had the nerve to say that he didn't need no dyke bi*ch defending him. He said this in front of the whole club. It didn't seem to bother Bea cause she knew he was drunk. She told the bartender not to serve him anymore.

"This bi*ch can't tell me what to do! I'm the boss of this operation!" He was clearly drunk and talking out of his mind. Cathy grabbed Bea and walked her back over to our section. Bea was always there for James and really had his back.

After the commotion died down, the band started playing again and folks started dancing and acting like nothing had happened. People stayed right up until 2:00 a.m. The lights came on and everything and people still weren't trying to leave. The bouncers had to start moving

people to the door before the police came and started messing with folks and Jake.

I noticed that James was still at the bar and he didn't look like he was in good shape. He was falling all off the stool and talking to himself. Jake saw me looking worried about him and told me that he'd make sure he got home safely. I hugged Jake and thanked him. Jake had one of his friends take me and Cicely home. Betty, Burt and Walter had already left. When we were pulling off, Cathy came up to the car and asked if she could get dropped off at her and Bea's place because she couldn't find Bea.

CHAPTER 30

My Worst Nightmare

WE LAUGHED AND TALKED ALL THE WAY TO MY HOUSE. Cicely, or Sugie, as we teased her, was really happy. She was excited that she was doing a good job with the business and about opening the new place.

Once we got to my house, I asked, "So who's going to church with me in the morning?" I knew they weren't going but just wanted to hear their excuses.

Cathy said, "Do you want the church to burn to the ground?" We laughed until I almost peed on myself.

Then Cicely said, "You know your brother Deacon Walter May will be there!" We all just got quiet.

"Can y'all believe what a change he's made since he's been in Philly?" I asked.

"No girl, I ain't never thought he would be nuthin!" said Cicely.

He was in the lounge tonight and didn't have one drink and was ready to go early because he had to be at church in the morning.

Cathy said, "Momma is so proud."

"I'm proud of Walter too, but I'm real proud of

Momma!" I said.

Cathy asked me why I was proud of Momma. Was it just for moving to Philly?

"Y'all know she been going out with Mr. Edwards from the church?"

They both said, "Whattt?"

Cicely said, "How long this been going on?"

I said, "About two weeks now. She says he's real nice and treats her nice."

Cathy said, "It's about time something nice happened for her, she had a rough life." She said, "I wonder if Momma giving up some pu**y?" She laughed, but Cicely and me just looked at her.

I said, "Everybody ain't like you Cathy, just give it up so quick!"

She said, "Sh*t, the apple don't fall too far from the tree! Momma ain't no angel. Word had it that she was runnin with Bowlin James down home and what make me believe it is one day I picked up Lolo and Denise and they said Momma was in the barn wit Bowlin James for a long time and we couldn't go in there. I was sayin to myself, Momma handling her business!"

Cicely said, "Well that's all in the past, cause we is making a new life for us and our family." She said, "So get on outta here church lady so you can pray for all us!" She and Cathy started laughing. I rolled my eyes and got out the car. I blew two kisses and walked to the house.

They waited until I got in and then they blew the

horn and pulled off. All the children were upstairs with Momma, so I turned off the nightlight and went in the room to get in the bed. I was tired and my feet were hurting from all that dancing. I was smiling thinking about all the fun we had at Jake's, and I knew that when they opened up the new place, it was gonna be even better.

I must have been sleep for about twenty minutes or so when I heard someone ringing the doorbell and the way they were ringing it was like they was the police. It scared me half to death! I turned on the light and got my robe. I went over to the door and asked who was there? They just kept ringing on the bell and knocking even harder! Now I was really scared. I didn't have any idea who it could be. My heart was beating out my chest and I was clinching my butt cheeks to keep from sh*tting on myself! I grabbed the bat that I kept by the door and I went over to the window. They were still ringing on the bell and knocking on the door. I didn't want Momma and the kids to wake up and come to the window or downstairs to the other door. I peeked out the curtain making sure that whoever was at the door couldn't see me. When I looked, it was James!

I closed the curtain fast. *What in the world was he doing here? How did he even know where I lived? I thought I was dead to him? Is his ass drunk? Does he think his drunk ass is getting some pu**y? And why is he ringing my doorbell like someone is chasing him? Is someone chasing him?*

He was ringing the doorbell even more so I flung

open the door ready to cuss his ass out or beat him with the bat and he fell in the house and onto the floor. That's when I could see that he was bleeding! I started screaming. I kneeled down on the floor and turned him over and picked his head up in my lap, his eyes were rolling back in his head! I start screaming even more, "What happened? Who did this to you?!" Blood was coming out his mouth.

"Clara, listen to me…" He could barely talk and his voice was soft like a whisper. I put my ear close to his mouth so I could hear him better.

"Jake is dead at the lounge. Bea shot us and Jake is dead. She thought I was dead too." He was choking on his blood. I tried to lift his head up more so he could get some air to breathe. I was saying "stay with me," and "keep talking baby." I was screaming, "Help Me! Help Me!"

"Bea stole all the money from Jake and Me and the house that I was buying for us! He was starting to take long deep breaths and more blood was coming out of his mouth and ears. He was hardly whispering now and he said, "I love you Clara. Bea killed us."

"No, please talk to me! Don't stop talking! James! James! Don't leave me like this!"

By now, Momma, Walter, and the children were standing around us. They're all screaming because James was bleeding all over me. There was a pool of blood on the floor and they didn't know if I was hurt too. The way I was screaming you might have thought I was shot.

Right then, James took his last breath. I saw the life leave his body. I screamed and cried and just held him. I was rocking back and forth and holding onto him.

"No, No, No! Don't leave me like this!" I couldn't believe that James was dead in my arms. I couldn't believe who he'd said did it! I hadn't felt this kind of pain since the loss of my first child. My heart was aching and I felt like the life was sucked out of me. My body shook and I felt chills all over. I looked down at James and his eyes were looking right at me, so I took my fingers and closed his eyelids. I kissed his forehead and started crying again. Why would she do this to you? I must have sat there for ten minutes just holding him and talking to myself. Momma and them just watched and nobody said one word.

The next thing I remember was Walter coming over to me and saying, "Come on Clara, he's gone. He's in a better place."

But was he? Did he know the Lord? It was like I was outside of my body. Nothing seemed real. By now, the police had arrived and they wanted to ask me some questions. I looked at my nightgown and it was covered in blood. Without warning, I threw up all over the floor. The blood was so thick and fresh that I could smell it. It made me think about what Cousin Dave had done to me. I told the police I had to get out of my gown and take a shower before I could talk to them.

Momma said, "Go on, get in the shower baby!" Her

eyes were so sad. Walter May said he would clean up the mess by the time I got out the shower. He said, he tried to move James' car out of the middle of the road, but he couldn't find the keys.

I went in the bathroom and turned on the shower and when I got in, I just bit into the rag and screamed as loud as I could. I couldn't believe that Bea would kill James. But was I sure that he said Bea shot him and killed Jake? Oh sh*t! Is Jake dead too? I hadn't even thought about that. But if Bea killed them, what would she do to me and my sisters? My heart was pounding and I felt like I was going to faint. How did James drive over here in that condition? What is Bea going to think when she finds out he died here? I can't tell anybody what James told me until I can figure out a plan to get us away from her.

I stayed in the shower for what seemed like an hour because I was shaking like a leaf and I was trying to get my thoughts together to talk to the police. Finally, I got myself together and when I got out the shower, I thought I heard Bea in the front room talking to the police. I got real quiet and cracked the door. When I heard her voice, I peed all down my leg. I closed the door quietly and leaned my back against the door and slid down to the floor. What the hell is she doing here? I was really shaking now. Did she follow James here? Did she see him talking to me? I was scared as sh*t. That's when I heard Momma call me.

"Clara you alright?"

"Yes, Momma! I'm coming!"

"Okay, the police want to ask you some questions and Bea is here."

Momma didn't know about Bea and Cathy. Cathy acted like Bea was just a friend of James that we all hang around. Momma had no idea that Cathy lived with her. She thought Cathy stayed with Gladys.

"Okay!"

What am I going to say? I can't let Bea know that I know nothing. I cleaned up the bathroom and got myself together and decided I was going to say that he was dead when I opened the door.

When I went back out there, they were putting the sheet over James' body. I started crying all over again. Bea came over to me and she had tears in her eyes and tried to hug me and I just turned and ran over to the stretcher that they put James on and started screaming and yelling. I didn't want her to touch me.

Walter came and got me and said, "Clara you gonna have to get it together and talk to the police so you can help them find out who did this to James."

That's when Bea said, "Yes, did he say anything? Did he say who did this to him?" She was trying to look like she had some tears in her eyes but she was looking real nervous to me, like she didn't know if I knew anything and was gonna tell the police. All kinds of thoughts ran through my mind, but I said, "No, he was dead when I

opened the door!" And I started crying all over again. Bea kept on with the questions.

"He didn't say anything?" She was starting to look relieved but trying to act sad.

"No!" She was asking more questions than the police. That's when my brother told her that was enough questions. You could tell that he didn't like Bea too much. I think he knew that her and Cathy was more than friends. The police didn't really care about a Black man getting killed. They asked a few questions and then left. They told us to notify the next of kin and they wanted me to come down to the police station in the morning to answer some more questions. But I didn't know any of his family, so Bea said she'd handle everything.

CHAPTER 31

Our Lives Were Changed Forever

THINGS WERE SETTLING DOWN. WALTER HAD CLEANED UP all the blood off the floor and threw out my nightgown. The house smelled like Clorox, Momma and the kids went back upstairs to bed, and everybody else was just sitting around looking at me. I could still smell fresh blood. I'll never forget that smell. I started thinking about what James told me about Jake. If Jake is dead, then I know what James said was true. I kept thinking how did Bea know to come to my house? My mind was racing. I couldn't believe that James took his last breath in my arms and the person that he said killed him is sitting in my living room. But how did James know where I lived? All these unanswered questions had me a nervous wreck and I guess the six cups of black coffeee that I drank didn't help the matter.

All of my sisters were at my house within the hour. Momma had called them. They couldn't believe what had happened to James. Cathy was really upset because she was real close to him since she was always around him, she cried and cried. The sun was coming up and I knew

I had to figure out a way to get up to Jake's cause if what James had told me was true, his body was just up there rotting. I had to think of a reason to get up to Jake's. I told them that I left my purse up at Jake's last night and I needed to give the police my ID. Bea said, "Clara, you should be resting. Don't worry about your ID. I'll-," and before she could finish, I said, "Look, I need to get out of this house!"

Cicely said, "Come on, if she need to get out this house, then she gonna get out!"

Bea looked like she got pale in the face. She said that she would stay with Momma and the kids. Burt and Jeff said that they'd stay there too and make sure the children got something to eat. That made me feel easy, cause Bea wasn't staying around my family by herself! Walter May came with us.

We all got in the car with Cicely's friend that had brought her to the house. We were all quiet on the ride there and I just kept crying every time I thought about James. Cicely said, "Jake don't even know about James yet. He said he was staying with me last night but he never came." When she said that, I got the most sickening feeling in my stomach and I told the man to pull over. I opened the door and threw up. My sisters were real sweet. They were rubbing my back and telling me that I was going to be alright. Once I got myself together, I must have looked like a piece of cotton, cause all the color had left me. I didn't know what I was going to do if Jake was

in his place dead.

When we pulled up, I was shaking and looking so nervous they kept asking me what's wrong? I said that I just felt funny because this was the last place that I had seen James alive. When we walked up, the door was locked like normal, but there was blood all over the doorknob.

Cicely said, "What the hell is all this blood all over the door?"

Walter May grabbed his hankerchief and wiped and unlocked the door with Cicely's keys. We all were walking in real slow and we were all close together. My heart was about to jump out my chest and my body was shaking so bad my sisters had to help me walk. Cicely was turning on the lights and the place was still a mess from the night before. Then she noticed a trail of blood that was from the front to the back! When I saw this, I knew that what James said was true. Cicely was heading to the back and so I said, "Walter May go on back there with her."

Before he could get back there, Cicely was screaming at the top of her lungs and running out from the back. She knocked Walter May down to the ground running from what she'd seen. She was screaming that Jake was dead. That somebody had shot him in the head!

The next thing I knew, they were slapping my face and throwing water on me. Walter was holding my head screaming, "Clara, is you alright? Wake up! Can you hear me?" All I heard was screaming and crying.

"Girl, you fainted. Is you okay?" My head was

pounding! I nodded that I was okay, but everything was spinning, nothing seemed real. I was looking around because I didn't know where I was. Walter sat me on the couch and then he went to tend to Cicely because she was losing it. She was at the bar pouring herself tall glasses of whiskey and drinking them down like water! Walter grabbed the bottle from her.

Betty was in the back, seeing if he had a pulse, she was a nurse now so she wasn't shocked to be around dead bodies. Cathy was over at the garbage can throwing up and Mally and Ernestine was standing there hugging each other and crying. Gladys was on her knees praying. This was not happening. Just last night we were all in here having so much fun and now two men that we knew and loved were gone.

Once the police left and Jake's body was picked up, we closed up Jake's Lounge and it never opened again. Ever.

Cicely was a nervous mess! She would only sleep for a couple of hours and pop right back up. She was scared that whoever did this to Jake might come for her. She didn't know if it was Warren because she had cut him a few months back or if it was one of the bar owners from the neighborhood. She went and got all of her stuff from the apartment and she never went back there again. It turned out that whoever robbed Jake got away with over twenty thousand dollars. Cicely said that he kept a safe in the lounge and that it was open and empty. All the money

they made and had saved for the new place was gone. She said she had some money that he kept at the house and some money that she had put aside. We always were taught, "It was a poor mouse that has one hole."

Within one week before we could even have the funeral for James, Cicely took Benji and they moved back to the country. Elleeboo and Juanita managed to talk me into letting them go back and stay with Cicely in the country. After what they'd seen, I knew they needed a change. They were going to stay on the farm for a couple of weeks until she found a little house to buy over in Warsaw.

Now that Cicely was back in Hustle and Jake's was closed, things weren't the same anymore. It was a sadness that hovered around me everyday. I hadn't seen my sisters since James' funeral, over a month ago. I hadn't been around Cathy and Bea. They moved into a new house over in Williamstown, New Jersey and Denise and Lolo were living with them. I kept thinking that was the house that James told me she stole from him. It seemed like everything that James told me before he died was right on. Jake was dead, Bea got a house in New Jersey. Her and Cathy got brand new cars and Ernestine had told me that Bea bought Cathy a diamond ring and they had all this fancy furniture!

The thing that hurt me the most, she didn't even

give James a decent funeral. Come to find out, James' momma and poppa didn't want nothing to do with him because of the life he chose. His poppa was a preacher and his momma taught the Sunday School. He had one older brother and he was real deep into the church too and hadn't seen him in over fifteen years. So, none of them came to collect the body and didn't come to the funeral. Bea had him buried in a pine box and had a viewing at Carl May's funeral home. There were only a few people that attended the funeral, me, my sisters, Momma, Walter May, Burt, Jeff, and a few people that he ran numbers with. The lady that said James was the father of her daughter came with the cutest little girl that looked just like him to pay their respects. How could he deny that little girl? She was the spitting image of him.

It was real sad that I was with him all that time and didn't know any of this about him. It was even sadder for Cathy. She took James' death real hard cause she was around him so much. But this was the day that Momma found out her and Bea was lovers and disowned her. One thing about Momma, she was traditional in her ways. She didn't believe in none of that funny business.

The story Momma told was that she was in the toilet stall and Bea and Cathy came in. She said that they didn't bother to see if anybody was in the there. Cathy was crying and carrying on and Bea was trying to comfort her and telling her not to worry that she didn't have to be scared. She told her that they were out of Philly and that

she would always protect her and the kids. She said Bea told Cathy that she loved her and Cathy said she loved her too. That's when Momma said she couldn't take it no more and she bust out the toilet stall and Bea and Cathy was standing there hugging and kissing like a man and woman.

She said before she knew it, she was slapping Cathy all in her head and quoting scriptures from the Bible. We heard her yelling, "Is this what you left you husband for? To come up here and blaspheme God?"

That's when we all went running to the toilets. Momma was swinging on Cathy and cussing Bea out. We all grabbed Momma and tried to calm her down. The look on her face was one that I had never seen, not even when we were back in Hustle and having all those babies. Momma looked like she was tired and full of disgust and hurt.

She asked Cathy and Bea, "Don't you know God destroyed Sodom and Gomorrah because men was with men and women was with women?" She looked at all of us and said to us. "I don't know what you gals done came up to Philly and got yourselves mixed up in, but I don't want nuthin to do with it. You gals done forgot everything that Revereand Waller preached to yall!" She told Cathy, "As long as you wit this woman, you is no longer my chile!" Then she grabbed her purse and told Walter May to take her home. In her face, you could see hurt as tears rolled down her cheeks. Cathy started

crying. As tough as she tried to be, she always had a soft spot for Momma.

We never did find out when the funeral services were held for Jake or if there was one. It wasn't even in the obituary section of the newspaper. I wonder if he even had family?

When it rains, it pours. Tuesday, November 1st, one week before my birthday, is a day I'll never forget. I was trying to get back to normal. I hadn't been to work in a week and Mr. Silverstein hadn't been coming in because he was taking care of Mrs. Silverstein. When I got into the office, it was pitch dark. I opened up the curtains and turned on the lights. I jumped back and almost had a heart attack! Mr. Silvestein was sitting over in the corner and he didn't look too good. I started walking over to him and I could smell him before I reached him. He smelled like he'd fallen off a whiskey truck.

"Mr. Silverstein, are you alright?" I kneeled down next to him to try to sit him up.

"Miriam died last night!" He started weeping like his heart was broke.

Even though Mr. Silverstein and me did what we did, I always knew he loved his wife and family. I didn't say anything, I just hugged him as tight as I could so that he knew I understood his pain.

"Clara, I did everything I could to keep her alive,

treatments, specialists, everything, but there was nothing they could do!"

He was sobbing and tears and snot were running down his face. "I've depleted our savings trying to get her better. I have drained all of the money out of the business! Everything I ever worked for, I gave to try to save her… and nothing worked!"

After about five minutes of him crying and me just trying to comfort him, he said, "Clara, I'm so sorry!"

"You don't have to apologize to me."

"I do! There's something that I have to tell you." I got real nervous.

"What is it?"

He looked down at the ground and said, "I have to close the business."

My heart sank to my stomach and felt like it was about to come out my butt!

"With all of the medical bills and treatments, I had to use all the money from the business and there's nothing left." He started crying again. "Miriam's insurance money is all that I have so I'm going to take that and retire to Florida."

He said that he'd been thinking about what he would do once she died and that he knew he couldn't stay in Philly cause it would just be too hard on him with all of the memories.

I told Mr. Silverstein that I understood that he had to do what was good for him. I told him that he had

been mighty good to me, in fact, better than my own kin. I appreciated everything he had done for my family. I assured him that I was going to be okay and would find another job. I let him know that I was a saver and that I had a little piece of change thrown to the side for a rainy day. I tried to smile but I felt like my world was coming down around me. I was scared because I was the one who took care of the family. I had a mortgage to pay. *Lord, what am I going to do?* My mind was in a daze.

"The office is closing at the end of the week, so I need you to start calling all of our customers and referring them to Allen Jacoby, his office is not too far from here." He went on to say, "Clara, I just want you to know that I love you." He reached out to hug me and I went over and hugged him and told him that I loved him too. That was the last time that I ever saw Mr. Silverstein!

For the entire night, I cried. I knew Momma wanted to go back down home with Cicely but she stayed because she didn't want to leave me by myself with all that had just happened. I told her about Mr. Silverstein closing the office and I just cried all night. Momma knew how much I had been through so she slept in the bed with me and hugged me. I knew it broke her heart to see me going through this because I could hear her crying and sniffling too.

I went to work the next few days and got everything ready to close down. I called all of the customers and sent them over to Jacoby Insurance. I packed up all of

the papers and had them mailed to Mr. Jacoby. I cleaned up and waited for the new people that were taking over the office to come get the keys. When they got there, I gave the man the keys. I walked around the office one last time and thanked God for all the good things that came from me working there. I sat at my desk one last time and spun around in the chair just like I did the very first day I walked into Silverstein's Insurance Company. Thinking about that day made me smile. I grabbed my box of belongings and when I left out that day, I never went back past there again.

I Needed A Break

I COULDN'T GET PAST THE SADNESS. I HADN'T GOTTTEN dressed in about two weeks. Momma kept asking me day and night if I was eating cause she said I was getting too skinny and my head was starting to look big. I told her that I just wasn't feeling like myself. I hadn't started looking for another job. I was just doing a lot of nothing.

Then Momma said, "Why don't we go down home for a couple of weeks?"

"Momma, I don't know."

"We ain't got to stay on the farm. We can stay at Cicely's place over in Warsaw?" I thought about it and it wasn't a bad idea.

Momma and me planned to leave that next week. I was starting to feel a little better thinking about getting away from Philly for a minute. Plus, I could see the kids and get a chance to clear my mind and not think about James and Mr. Silverstein.

Walter May seen us off on the Greyhound. We told him that we'd be back in a couple of weeks. When the bus pulled off, it was the same feeling I had when I was on

the bus leaving Hustle for the first time, like all my cares was rolling away. For the first time in weeks, I fell asleep. I didn't wake up until Momma was shaking me saying, "Gal, we here!"

I jumped up rubbing my eyes and stretching and said, "We here already. I just closed my eyes for a minute!" Momma said, "Gal you slept and snored like a hog the whole way down the road!" I asked why didn't she wake me up.

"Gal, you ain't slept in weeks and it caught up to you. You needed it. I ain't seen you that peaceful in weeks!"

Since we had made plans so fast, we hadn't even told anybody that we were coming, we were just showing up. We had to hitch a ride to Cicely's house from the bus stop. This was common around home, people didn't mind giving you a ride. Cicely didn't live but five minutes from where the bus dropped us off in Warsaw, we could have walked but some nice man asked us where we was heading. He happened to be heading in that direction and knew Cicely. I wasn't surprised that he knew Cicely. She hadn't lived in Warsaw but two months and already men knew her. When she saw us get out of his car, she came running out the door. She was yelling, "What is y'all doin here?"

The house was cute as can be. It sat back off the road a bit and was a light gray color with a closed-in porch and a little shed on the side. She had two big bushes in the front and a cornfield on the side and across the street. She

also had one of those ditches in the front to catch the rain that I almost fell in because I wasn't paying attention. She came and hugged Momma and me.

"I'm so glad y'all is here! Y'all come on in! The chilren is at school. They is gonna be so glad to see y'all too!" She fixed us something to eat and we just sat and talked.

When the children were coming up the road, we could hear them laughing and talking all loud. They seemed like they were getting along good in Warsaw. They weren't giving Cicely any trouble and were even doing well in their classes. When they came in and saw us, they were happy at first and came up and gave us hugs.

Then Juanita said, "Momma, me and Eldridge ain't goin back to Philly!"

"I'm not here to take y'all back. I'm here to get some peace and quiet!" She looked at me and then she hugged me again. I guess she felt sorry for me after all I had been through.

They filled us in on all that was going on. Benji had a girlfriend named Sandy. It was hard to believe that he was coming up on sixteen years old. He was right bashful so he was denying it, but I could tell by the way he was smiling that it was true. They seemed to be adjusting well. They had been through so much so young that it was good to see them happy for once.

I was down there for about a week and I was just thinking about what I was going to do next. I didn't have a job but I did have a little money saved up that I could

use to pay my mortgage for about six months before I would have to bring in some money, so I wasn't worried about that. I just could not stop thinking about Bea killing James and Jake.

Later on that night, me and Cicely was sitting on the porch by ourselves and I said, "Cicely do you ever wonder who killed James and Jake? Do you think it was the same person?"

She took a long, deep breath and said, "At first, I thought it was Warren. Then, I thought it might have been a hit that the Mafia put out on him for some other stuff. But when James ended up dead at your house and the last place that we seen both of them was at the lounge, I started to think that something wasn't right!" She looked at me and she got real serious and said, "I believe the same person killed them both!"

"Why you think that?"

"Cause anytime James was last at the bar, he always waited for Jake to lock up and they would leave together." That was true. They were really cool and James always watched Jake's back and vice versa. I knew even more now that what James told me before he died had to be true.

"But girl, I try not to think about that no more. That's in the past and I'm looking toward the future!" She got real chile like and said, "I met a man!"

"You met a man already?"

"Yeah girl, he one of the Barker boys from over in Sharp!"

"Them fine brothas that got the Negro League baseball team?"

"Yes, girl! Henry Barker! He is tall, dark, and real handsome. He got them pretty white teeth and girl he got a gold one on the side!" She was so giddy! Cicely always knew that she was coming back to the country, that's why she didn't want to buy a house in Philly.

"If he has one of those gold teeth, he must be sharp!"

"Girl, he is! This the man I'm gonna marry!"

Since we been grown, I hadn't heard Cicely talking about getting married. This one must be real special.

A few days later she said, "We's going on a double date tonight."

"Girl, I ain't in no mood to go on a date."

"Well get in one cause Henry and his brother is pickin us up at 7pm."

"I didn't bring clothes to be going on a date."

She looked at me like I was crazy. Like I didn't know about all the beautiful clothes she had.

We had a really nice time. I think John Wayne and me hit it off better as friends. Don't get me wrong, he was a fine Barker boy. I just wasn't ready to open myself up for that and I was leaving to go back to Philly the next week.

I went over to Hustle to visit Hamilton and Margaret and their four beautiful children. Margaret cooked up some good food and me and Hamilton talked all day.

He gave me some good advice on how to move on. He was such a good brother. Now I was feeling like I could go back to Philly. I ended up being down home for three weeks, but I think I spent two of the weeks just sleeping and resting. Momma decided she was staying for awhile and I thought that was best too. Walter May worked a lot and I think she liked being there with the children more than anything.

CHAPTER 33

Puttin On My Big Girl Panties

I HAD BEEN RUNNING FROM MY PAST AND NOW IT WAS TIME to go home and put on my big girl panties. I had to find a job and get on with my life. When I got back, the first thing I did was check in with all of my sisters. I called Ernestine first and of course she was at work and Jeff wasn't home either so this was my chance to talk to lil Cicely about what she had told Juanita that day when we were all out.

I started by telling her that what we talked about was just between us and that we couldn't tell Ernestine or Jeff what we talked about. I hated having to do this because this child was already holding enough secrets, but I wanted her to trust me. She said real soft, "Okay." I reminded her about that day when we were all up at the restaurant near the Robert Wood Home and that I had over heard her say the Jeff was touching her bookie. It was silence on the other end of the phone. I told her that she wasn't in any trouble and that if he was touching her that it wasn't her fault. She was still silent on the phone. I told her that she didn't have to say anything right now, but

that I was gonna come get her on the weekend to go get some ice cream and we would be able to talk more then. I knew in my gut that the bastard was touching on her that's why he was always picking her up and taking her around everywhere with him. She seemed excited when I said that we were going to get ice cream. That was the first time that she said more than two words on the phone. "Okay, I'm gonna tell Momma Jimmie that we going to get ice cream!" She and Butchie Boy called Ernestine, Momma Jimmie. Then she hung up the phone.

I called Gladys and she didn't answer and I knew Mally was working. I was starting to get that lonely feeling that I had before I went down to Cicely's. Betty was my last call. I called and she answered on the second ring. It was good to hear her voice. She asked me how I was doing and all about Cicely's new house. She told me that Burt had been asking about me and was wondering when I was coming back.

"Oh really?" I asked her, "Why he'd want to know when I was coming back? Had he heard anything about who killed James and Jake?"

"No, he said they are hiring at Bell Atlantic and he can get you a job."

When I heard her say that, I dropped the phone and did a Holy Ghost dance! When I picked up the phone again, I could hear her calling my name, "Clara, Clara? Are you there?"

"Sorry girl, I just caught the Holy Ghost!" She told

me that she would have Burt call me when he came home.

Burt called me and did just what he said he was going to do. He got me an interview with Bell Atlantic Phone Company. This was a good job and it was only a few Black folks working up in there. Word had it that you had to pass the paper bag test which meant if you were darker than a paper bag, your ass wasn't getting the job. I knew I wasn't going to have a problem in that area.

When I walked in on the day of the interview, they thought I was white. I could tell by how nice they were treating me. They asked if I wanted some water while I waited and kept smiling at me. When it was my turn to go in to meet with the supervisor, I was nervous. On the way back to his office, the lady walking me back said, "Don't worry, he hires all the pretty white woman," and she winked at me. I said, "Oh, okay!" And I winked right back.

I had made up mind a long time ago that if passing for white was going to get me further along, then I was just gonna let them think that. When I got into the next room, the lady said, "He'll be right with you, but please fill out this paperwork while you wait."

On the paper, they asked your name, address, previous employers, if you had a high school diploma, your race, and a bunch of other stuff. I got real nervous cause I knew that I didn't have a high school diploma,

so I prayed to God. *God, you know I need this job. I don't like to lie, but I'm going to have to check the box that says I have a high school diploma and I know I don't. I also want to check the box that says I'm white but that would be double lies, so Father please forgive me in advance!* After my prayer, I could only bring myself to check the box that said I graduated from high school.

"Clara Johnson, Mr. Carmichael will see you now." I hadn't even finished filling out the paperwork. When I went in the office, there was an older white gentleman sitting at a desk. He had on glasses and a suit with a bow tie. He looked at me and said, "Hi Ms. Johnson. My name is Mr. Carmichael, please have a seat."

"Pleased to meet you!"

He asked for the paperwork that I was filling out so I gave it to him. He started looking it over and says, "So I see here that you worked for an insurance company for four years?"

"Yes, sir!"

"What were your daily responsibilities?" I told him that I pretty much did everything. I started off as a receptionist and worked my way up to being the office manager. I talked about everything I did working for Mr. Silverstein.

He was still looking over the paperwork and said, "You forgot to check your race so I'll just check white for you."

I started to say something, but then I figured that

God had worked it out without me having to lie. He then asked me how soon I could start.

"Tomorrow?"

He said, "Perfect, you're hired! Be here tomorrow at 8:00 a.m. sharp for training!"

He stood up, shook my hand, and said, "Welcome to the Bell Atlantic Family. Tracy will go over your salary and benefit package tomorrow!"

I didn't even know what a salary and benefit package was but I smiled and said, "Thank you sir!" I knew I could find out later on from Burt all the stuff that I didn't know.

The God I serve is good like that. When one door closes, another opens! I prayed and thanked God for always watching out and protecting me.

That night, I called and thanked Burt for getting me the interview. He was happy that things had gone good. I asked what a salary and a benefit package was and he said that my salary is the money that I make in a year and that the benefit package is retirement plan and insurance plan so if I get sick and need to go to the doctor or if I needed to go to the dentist, that Bell Atlantic pays for their employees. I couldn't believe it! I had never heard of nothing like that. This was better than I thought. I was excited and got in the bed early that night so I wouldn't be late or tired for my first day at Bell Atlantic!

After the first day of work, I knew I was going to be there the rest of my working life. I loved it and the people were very nice to me. I had finally found where I

belonged.

I finally spoke to Ernestine who was working her way up too. She had gotten a promotion and was the shift manager and working long hours. I told her about my new job at Bell Atlantic and I told her that I wanted to come and take lil Cicely out for ice ream on Saturday and she said it was fine.

When I got there on Saturday and rang the bell, Butchie boy came to the door. He hugged me and was happy to see me. We went in the house and I asked him where was lil Cicely and he said she was upstairs with Daddy Jeff. I called up the stairs for lil Cicely to come down and when she came down she was kind of sheepish and gave me a half way hug. Then Jeff came down. He hugged me and said, "Hey Clara, it sure is good to see you! What you doing down the bottom?"

I gave him a funny look and said, "I'm here to take lil Cicely to get ice cream. Ernestine did't tell you?"

He scratched his head and said, "No, she must have forgot." Then he said, "But lil Cicely ain't feelin too good today that's why she was upstairs laying down."

He gave her a look and said, "Isn't that right Cicely?" She looked confused and said softly, "Yes sir."

I knew something was going on with this girl because she loved ice cream. He told me that Butchie Boy is feeling fine he can go. I was pissed. The look I gave him let him know that I wasn't a fool. So I took Butchie Boy and we went and got some ice cream. This thing was

worrying me sick! I knew that he knew that I was onto him and he was gonna keep lil Cicely away from me to keep the truth from coming out. I prayed and prayed that God would do something to help lil Cicely. I called every week to try to get her or see her, but there was always an excuse.

A couple of months had passed and Momma called and told me that Ernestine was coming down there and bringing Butchie Boy and lil Cicely to stay with them for a little while. She didn't get into why, but said she was leaving Jeff because he wasn't no good. I thought maybe Ernestine found out that he was touching that girl. Maybe that's why she was always so mean to Lil Cicely. I remember a while back, Ernestine had borrowed Jeff's car and we were gonna take the children to get some ice cream and lil Cicely got excited, she couldn't have been no more than six or seven at the time and she sat up and said, "Momma Jimmy, is I'm gonna get some ice cream?"

Ernestine took the back of her hand and slapped the girl so hard she fell back on the seat! It pissed me off and hurt my feelings. I yelled at Ernestine and said, "Why did you hit the girl in her face like that? All she did was ask you a question!"

"Don't worry bout how I whoops my chilren!" Me and Ernestine was about to fight that day. Then she had the nerve to tell her to shut up all that hollering after she damn near knocked her head off. Nobody got ice cream that day and I left and didn't come back around

for months!

If she did find out what Jeff was doing, we'd never know the truth. She wasn't the type to put her business out there and it didn't seem like Lil Cicely was gonna tell it either cause she didn't have anyone that she trusted enough except Juanita. In these days, this type of stuff happened all the time. It wasn't like the men ever got in trouble for it either. It was just how things were. I was happy that they were all going to be together again, but this time, they weren't dirt poor. We had finally made a better life for the family!

CHAPTER 34

Time Waits For No One

IT DIDN'T SEEM LIKE TEN YEARS HAD ALREADY GONE BY! After Momma died five years ago, it seemed like the family just went in different directions. Everybody was doing their own thing.

Cathy and Bea were still together living over in Williamstown. Bea had started some new businesses and it was rumored that she had killed a few more people to get them. They say she killed a white man that she was friends with and stole his business from under him and did the same thing a few years later to her friend that owned a placed where they fix cars. I guess after she got away with killing James and Jake, it became easy for her. The day Momma found out about Cathy and Bea was the last time they ever spoke. My Momma wasn't no angel but she believed that woman and woman being together was a sin and that it said so in the Bible.

Cathy believed that Momma wrote a letter and told Paulie that Bea and Cathy slept in the same room and in the same bed. Paulie went up to Williamstown looking for Bea and Cathy and tried to get the children.

It was a big fuss. The police was called and Paulie ended up getting arrested. He stayed in jail about three months before they let him out. Momma and Ernestine got him a bus ticket and sent him back down to Virginia when they finally let him out. Cathy never let Denise and Lolo see Momma again.

What Cathy never knew is that Denise was the one that wrote her Poppa and told him everything, but Momma just let it go to protect Denise. Cathy was a mean and hateful person. She did come and bring the kids to Momma's funeral where she wanted to act a fool hollering and crying and chasing the casket out the church because she knew she was wrong for choosing a woman over her Momma. Denise hated her for being with a woman and for keeping them from seeing Momma and her poppa! Her and Lolo, or Lorenzo as they called him now, went to school with all white folks out in New Jersey. They would get teased and picked on a lot because they were Black and Bea was still acting and dressing like a man. This kind of living wasn't accepted in these times and people would throw stuff at the house and write mean stuff on the house and cars. It was hard for the children out there, but Cathy didn't care about that as long as she had money, clothes, cars, and jewelry. Cathy and Ernestine still saw each other because they were working at the same mental hospital somewhere in New Jersey.

When Ernestine left Jeff, she quit her job at the restaurant and started working at the hospital with Cathy.

She had moved and bought a house over in New Jersey in a town called Chesilhurst. She ended up moving with the man that was her neighbor on Holly Street when she was living with Jeff. I knew when I saw them at the lounge that night that they were more than friends. Now that she was really on her feet and had a house and a good man, Butchie Boy and Cicely was coming back to live with them and finish high school out there. Ernestine was also having another baby. She was dealing with Jeff and Cecil at the same time so she didn't really know who was the baby's daddy, but Cecil knew that and didn't care. He was going to raise the child like it was his even if it it wasn't.

When Cicely and Butchie Boy came back, he wasn't the sharpest knife in the drawer and so he dropped out of school and entered the US Army. The Army was recruiting colored boys to go fight in the Vietnam War left and right. After a year when he came back, he was a nut. He couldn't hold a job in a pie factory and all he did was drink himself crazy and run with women. By the time he was twenty-one, he had six kids with six different women and wasn't taking care of none of them. He was such a nice-looking man but wasn't worth sh*t. Lil Cicely finished high school and got a job at the Electric Company in New Jersey. She had a daughter with a guy from Philly named Bunky Salley, but that didn't last as long as the pregnancy. A couple of years later, she met a very nice man named Henry Sawyer. They dated for a year and then got married and moved to a house not

too far from Ernestine and Cecil's house in Chesilhurst. Ernestine had a son named Michael and a little girl, we call Patsy, by Cecil. Everybody seemed like they were doing real good out there too.

Cecil's heart had been bad for awhile and he had already had three heart attacks before but the last one took him on home to be with the Lord. He died right in their house on the toilet. Cathy, Gladys, and I came to his viewing and went back to Ernestine's after. The house was packed from all of the people coming by for the repass. They were bringing all kinds of foods and cakes. Some things just don't change no matter where you are, Black folks make sure to help out when somebody they know and love pass on.

Lil Cicely's husband Henry had cooked most of the food and boy could he cook. He told lil Cicely that he was going around the corner to their house to change his clothes and he'd be right back to help serve the food. He was such a nice man and treated lil Cicely like she was a flower, sweet and delicate. Everybody had come back to the house after the funeral service to show respect to Cecil. We were all sitting around talking and had forgot about the time, maybe an hour or so had passed by when we saw the police with their lights and sirens on pull into the yard. We were all wondering what they were here for. I remember Butchie Boy, who wasn't drunk yet was standing in the doorway.

They all knew the police officers in the town because

it was a small little country town. Butch said, "What's up Milton? You coming to pay your respects to Cecil?"

He took his hat off and said, "No, I need to speak to Cicely."

I'll never forget how pitiful he looked waiting for Cicely to come to the door. Butch called for Cicely. She had the strangest look on her face as she walked over to him. When she got there, he said, "Cicely, I'm so sorry to have to tell you this. There's been a really bad accident around the corner near the playground and I'm sorry, Henry didn't make it."

The next thing I saw was lil Cicely running down the street. Butch tried to catch her but she was running like a deer. We all jumped in the cars and went around there. When we got there, they were putting the sheet on him and she was leaning over him wailing. She kept saying, "Why? Why? We were moving next month! He was adopting Dawn! Why God? Why?" She was a mess. It brought back the pain of when James died in my arms. That pain feels like somebody knocking the wind out of you. They gave her a sedative to calm her down.

I took vacation time off from work and stayed with lil Cicely, nobody knew what she was going through like I did. She would sit and stare at the walls. She wouldn't eat anything and she'd cry all day. The only time she managed to get herself together is when Dawn came around. She loved that little girl to pieces and was very protective of her. Once they got through burying Cecil,

they had a funeral for Henry. He was from Long Island, New York and didn't have many friends so they had a small ceremony. His body was cremated and his ashes were put over near Cecil's grave. They were really close so that made a lot of sense.

Big Cicely married Henry Barker and they started their family. She'd had two children with him already and the third was in the oven. Their oldest daughter caught menagitis when she was just a baby and lost her hearing and couldn't speak. But the other babies were just fine. Henry and Cicely had a nice family and did good for themselves. He worked in Washington, D.C. during the weekdays doing carpentry work. He owned a little fishing boat and he'd take out fishing parties on the weekend to make extra cash. Cicely worked at the Levi Company sewing jeans. Once she got married and started her family, it wasn't any room in the house for Momma, Juanita, and Eldridge. Juanita and Eldridge moved back to Philly and lived with me. Momma wanted to stay down south so she moved in with her cousin in Maryland, that's where she was living when she died.

Benji got married to the girl Sandy that he was dating since he was about fifteen or sixteen years old. They had two chilren together named Bunny and Chuckie, and lived in King and Queen County with Sandy's momma. Benji was working in Louisiana on the fishing boat for five years. He would be gone for ten months out of the year and then he'd come home for two months. Him and

Sandy were saving to buy a house. Big Cicely said that he would send every penny home to Sandy and that he would be out there living on next to nothing.

The last time he came home after being away for ten months, Cicely said that Sandy told him that he couldn't stay there no more and that she ain't want his simple ass no more. Folks had been telling Cicely that she was running with some guy and spending all the money Benji was sending home. They said she didn't have a dime of the money he had sent for them to buy a house. Cicely said she hadn't seen Benji this hurt since Momma had passed away. He went and stayed with Cicely and Henry for a week and the next weekend, went out to Sandy's momma's house and shot Sandy five times point blank range with a shotgun. Sandy's Momma, the kids, and everybody was there when he did it! Then he went on back to Cicely's house and told them what he did and waited for the police. He got twenty years in the state prison.

Mally had stopped coming around after all the bad stuff started happening. She ended up marrying her long-time boyfriend. She had one daughter and they moved somewhere near Yeadon, Pennsylvania, close to his family. She nor Fanny didn't even come to Momma's funeral because nobody knew how to get in contact with them.

CHAPTER 35

You Can Always Depend On Family

BETTY AND BURT WERE STILL TOGETHER. I SAW THEM ALL the time cause Burt and I worked together at Bell Atlantic. Their sons, Eddie and John, were some good-looking boys. John reminded me of Poppa and Walter when he was younger-always drunk! He didn't work and was spoiled rotten since he was the baby. Betty gave him any and everything he wanted. Eddie was my favorite nephew. He was always such a nice, well-mannered boy. He had a son with a girl from Germantown when he was only sixteen and then they had a baby daughter when he was only seventeen. He married her and they converted to Islam.

He was becoming more and more conscious of issues in our communities, always talking about how white people treated Black people and how we needed to rise up as a people. He would come by to see me from time to time and I would talk to him about God and tell him that God had a plan for his life. He was still my sweet Eddie and he always treated me with kindness and respect even though we had different views on God.

One night, it had to be about 2:00 a.m., someone was ringing my bell like crazy. It scared me so much and for a minute it took me back to when James was ringing my bell the night he was killed. I jumped up.

I didn't know anybody that could be ringing my bell this time of the morning. Juanita and Eldridge was grown now so they didn't live here anymore and the lady I rented the upstairs to was sweet as pie and wouldn't have anyone that would be coming here this time of morning either. So, I went and looked out the curtain and it was Eddie. He looked scared to death! He was sweating and dressed in all black. All I said is, "Lord, please not again!" I opened the door and he ran in the house.

"Boy, what is wrong with you?"

"Aunt Clara, I messed up real bad!" He was pacing the floor back and forth. He kept saying over and over again "Nobody was supposed to get hurt!"

I kept asking him what he was talking about? I was getting scared, the palms of my hands were sweating and I was shaking like a leaf. He looked at me with the most serious look and said, "I need to go in your basement."

"Boy what? Why you need to go in my basement?" Now I was looking at him like he was crazy.

"It's better that you don't know." The way his eyes was looking, I knew he was in trouble and it reminded me of what James used to say to me. I thought about it for a minute and I just turned my back. I heard him go down the stairs and I went and stood on the porch so I

wasn't tempted to go look. When he came back up, he hugged me and kissed me on my forehead. Then he put his hood on his head and left out the back door. It was all a flashback from James, from the things he was saying to the kiss on the forehead. I was a nervous mess.

The next morning, his face was all over the news and newspaper. They said on the news that he killed a police chief—shot him execution style while he sat in his car. They claimed he was the leader of a group called the Black Panther Party and they were a violent group that was responsible for a lot of killings in the city. They had a $5,000 reward for anyone that had information on him. I knew Betty and Burt had to be going crazy. I tried calling them but kept getting a busy tone. One thing you cannot do is kill a police officer. I went by their house but there was all kind of reporters staked out there and the shades were pulled so I just kept walking before they started asking me questions.

The police harassed Betty and Burt all the time. Bell Atlantic eventually fired him cause the police were always coming up to the job messing with him and questioning people in his department and telling them that Burt's son was a cop killer. They did the same thing to Betty until she was let go from the hospital. Burt had to pick up work as a janitor at a school and Betty had to start cleaning people's houses because nobody would hire them. Eddie was on the run for about four months before he turned himself in. While he was on the run, it was hell for Betty

and Burt, the police would come to their house all times
of the night, trash their home and flatten the tires on their
car. It got so bad that they sold the house and moved to
an apartment out in Delaware where nobody really knew
them.

I was beginning to get nervous. What if the police
found out that I was Betty's sister and came here and
started harassing me like they were doing to some of her
close friends? Eddie had been down in my basement. If
they came here, what would they find? I was too old to
be mixed up in this mess! I knew I had to go in that
basement and see what in the devil he went down there
for.

That night when I got home from work, the first
thing I did was head to the basement. I turned on all
the lights, got me a flashlight, and started looking. In my
heart, I knew I was looking for a gun, since they said the
Police Chief was shot in the head.

I had searched for hours and was about to give up.
I was sitting on the floor and I was praying, Lord, what
am I doing? I looked up at the ceiling and noticed one
of the panels wasn't quite lined up with the others. I got
the ladder from against the wall and set it up. Deep in
my heart I was hoping not to find nothing, but as I was
climbing up the ladder, my gut was telling me different.
I slid the panel back, and reached my hand up in the
ceiling and my heart seemed like it stopped. I was feeling
all around and then my hand made contact with the cold

metal. I knew it was the gun that he had put up there. What else could it be? I quickly moved my hand, put the panel back nice and neat, moved the ladder back, and ran upstairs.

Once the police had Eddie in custody, his lawyers said they beat him until you couldn't recognize him. He couldn't have visitors and there was no bail. In this town, there was no such thing as a fair trial for a Black man. If they said you did it, you were guilty. The trial was quick and even though he had an alibi and they never found the weapon, they sentenced him to life in prison without the possibility of parole. It killed Betty and Burt, the embarrassment and cold shoulder they got from people, made them stay in all the time. They would come outside to go to work, run their errands, and head right back home.

I never went down in the basement again, until later that year when I was going down home to Virginia to see Cicely at our family reunion. I don't think I had one good night's sleep in the house since I knew the gun was in there. Right before I was getting on the road, I went back in the basement and did the same routine that I did when I found the gun. Once I got it down, I made sure there wasn't any bullets in it, and wrapped it in a scarf and made sure all the fingerprints were wiped off. All of us knew how to use guns, I just never liked them. I put the gun in an old shoebox and packed it in the trunk of

my car. I made sure to drive the speed limit and prayed all the way to Virginia.

I finally crossed the Virginia state line and made it to the Tappahanock River Bridge. I pulled over on the side of the road and got the shoebox out of the trunk. I got back in my car and waited until it was nice and dark and there were no other cars going or coming across the bridge. I started driving across the bridge as I prayed to God to forgive me for my sins. Right when I got to the tallest part of the bridge, I opened the shoebox, took the gun out of the scarf, and tossed the gun out the window and down into the river. Relief came over me as I got that gun out of my house and life forever. I had the best time at the family reunion. Everybody came down to Cicely's house the third week of August for what had become the Fortune/Barker Family Reunion.

Walter May was still doing good living up in Philly. He didn't want to move back to Virginia when Momma and Cicely left. Since he was doing so well for himself he stayed. He still doesn't drink and has a good job at the warehouse. The boss there loves him and treats him like he was his son. He's still a deacon and member of National Temple Baptist Church and has quite a few women that he was rumored to be dating, some in the church and some out. He ended up marrying some crazy lady that wanted to control him and his money so that didn't last but a minute. He never had any children and still comes

by to take me to and from church every Sunday.

When Lolo, Cathy's son got big, he accused Walter May of touching him when he was a little boy. He told Cathy that when Walter May would come home drunk from hanging out that he would wake him up and make him suck his d**k.

Walter denied it but him and Cathy's relationship wasn't the same. She tried to run Walter May over with her car and she was blaming Momma. Momma was living when this happened but she never would address it. I don't know if it was because she and Cathy wasn't on speaking terms and she told Cathy she would never talk to her again as long as she was with Bea. Or if she just knew it was a flat out lie. I just don't believe Momma would have let that go on the way she's against any funny business with men and men and women and women. And because she was so protective over her grandbabies.

Carrie is still married to Robbie Reynolds. He still get drunk everyday and he still whippin her ass. She had four kids by him and lives down in Carat County right outside of Hustle. She works at the Levi factory too with Cicely. Carrie was such a pretty girl, I never knew what she saw in Robbie! He was mean as a black snake and looked like one too. Lucky that she was a pretty girl cause her kids turned out to be some attractive children. I'm glad they didn't take after their daddy's side of the family. Her youngest son had a terrible mouth on him and would talk to her any kind of way but the old folks say

what goes around comes around and that's what she get for the way she treated and talked to my Momma. Even though Carrie was a mean and hateful little hussy all her life, and didn't want to help nobody, I always felt sorry for her cause she was the only one of Momma's children that never left the country. None of my sisters would help her out when she fell on tough times, but she was my baby sister and I was gonna always have her back.

Our family had been through a lot. The kids had seen a lot and been bounced around a lot. Juanita and Eldridge came to live with me to finish out their last years of high school. Juanita and me never had a close relationship because she never really lived with me and I knew she hated me because of it so we made the best of it and stayed out of each other's way. I tried to make sure that she had everything that she needed, but she was so independent and wouldn't let me help her. She got a job when she was in the 12th grade and she told me that when she graduated, she was moving out. Two days after her graduation she moved out to a little apartment that she found on June Street. Juanita was real cute and was shaped real nice, all the men was always looking at her, so I knew she had some boyfriend that was helping her out. But like my Momma didn't ask me any questions about how I was getting things done, I didn't ask her any either.

After Eldrige graduated from high school, he worked odd jobs here and there. He got himself into some trouble too and had to go away to college, that's what we'd say

when one of our family members went to prison. He got in a bar fight and ending up hitting some fellow over the head with a bar stool and the boy died. I spent a pretty penny on lawyer fees to keep him from getting a first-degree murder charge. Lucky for me that this didn't come out right when it happened, it wasn't until three years later that they caught up with him. Another thing was that when Black people got killed, it wasn't all over the news and in the newspapers. They charged him with aggravated assault and he did two years upstate. When he came home, he married his girlfriend Naomi, and they had a little girl, I called Buttons. He brings her to visit me some Saturdays and we have lunch together.

ONE DAY AFTER WORK, I CAME HOME TO FIND A LETTER from the bank mixed in with the rest of the mail. I opened it quickly and there was a check along with the deed to the house! The letter said that I was finished paying for my house and I now owned it. Making those double mortgage payments and some triple payments really paid off. I was able to pay off my house in ten years! Mr. Silverstein really knew what he was talking about. I was so happy and thankful that I fell to my knees and praised God! To God Be the Glory!

I still work at Bell Atlantic as the Senior Customer Service Supervisor and I live at 4907 Cedar Avenue in West Philadelphia. I'm a member, trustee, and usher at National Temple Baptist Church. Everbody knows now that I am not white and that I'm a Black woman, and that I'm a Christian. No more half way living for the Lord, you can't sin Monday through Saturday and go to church on Sunday and call yourself a Christian… so no more pretending for me. Why should I have to pretend to be something I'm not? I have all of the pictures on my desk of my beautiful Black family members for everyone to see. Customers look surprised when they come to my

desk and I just say with a smile, that's my family. I LOVE James Brown's lyrics, "Say it loud! I'm Black and I'm Proud!"

STILL HUSTLING

An Exclusive Sneak Peek at Book 2 in the "Hustle" Series

INTRODUCTION

"I KNOW MY ID IS FROM MARYLAND, I JUST MOVED BACK TO Philly. I'm just trying to get my phone turned on. I gave you the address and here is my lease."

I could hear her from across the room. Peter was trying to explain that it was Bell Atlantic's policy for someone to have a Pennsylvania ID to apply for phone service. But she was not trying to hear what he was talking about. He finally got fed up and came over to me.

"Ms. Johnson, I have a lady at my desk and she is not understanding our policy about state identification. Can you please help her?"

Since I was the customer service manager, I always had to deal with the problem customers, or the Black customers that had a little too much bass in their voice and roll in their neck. Today I had a bad headache though and wasn't in the mood to hear a lot of noise. I took two aspirin and waited for her to come over to my desk. As she walked over, I heard her saying, "All of this. I'm just trying to get my phone turned on."

Once she reached my desk and I looked up, our eyes met and she looked like she saw someone from the dead. Her face looked familiar but I didn't remember from where. I've never been good with remembering faces. She

kept looking at me like I was a monster from a horror movie. She started backing up and then walked away. After stuttering a bunch, she said she'd come back another day. Just as she turned to leave, I remembered who she was. She was one of Sugie's girls from back at Jakes! As she headed towards the door, I got up and walked behind her.

"Gloria? Is that you?" She turned around and looked at me. The only thing in her eyes was fear. I took a few more steps in her direction.

"Umm, yes, it's me but I'm going to come back another time!" She was still trying to get to the door. For some reason, she didn't want to be bothered with me. I reached out for her hand.

"Gloria, it's okay. Don't leave, let me help you." I gave her a look that said, I'm going to take care of you. "Come, sit down and let me get your phone turned on." Hesitantly, she walked back over to my desk and sat down. All the attitude she had when she was over at Peter's desk had disappeared.

I hadn't seen Gloria in over ten years, since the night Jake's closed for good.

"Gloria, it's so good to see you! How've you been?"

She was still looking at me strangely like she was scared of me.

"I'm fine," she said as she sat trembling in front of me. By the way she was acting, I wasn't sure if she knew who I was or if she had me confused with someone else.

"Do you remember me? I'm Sugie's sister, Clara."

She nodded her head like she recognized me but she still wasn't receiving me as warmly as I had her. I started to feel uncomfortable with how she was looking at me.

"It's been a long time. I haven't seen you since the night that Jake's closed."

When I said that, her eyes got real big and she leaned in close and whispered, "Did James tell you who killed him?"

I almost fainted! Now I started trembling too. My hands started to sweat and my head started pounding even more. I don't know which was pounding more, my head or my chest. I was trying to answer but the words wouldn't come out. I looked at her the same way she had been looking at me. Is this girl crazy? Why is she asking me this? The only people that knew that James came to my house the night he died was my family. She could tell that she'd caught me off guard.

"I'll come back another day," she said as she jumped up and took off for the door. She was walking so fast, there was no way that I would catch her. Besides, I wasn't going to look like a fool chasing a customer.

All day it bothered me. Everyone around me could visibly see that I was shaken up. They kept asking if I was alright. I felt the same emotional drain as the night that James was killed. I was just trying to help Gloria get her phone turned on. I was not expecting to open this can of worms. That wasn't a normal question. Either she knew something, or she was crazy as hell. His murder

wasn't highly publicized because he was a Black man—a crooked one at that. The murders were never on the news or in the newspaper and nobody in law enforcement did anything to try to find the killer. The day we closed up Jake's, my family decided that we would not tell a soul that he came to my house and died. We told everyone that we found James and Jake dead inside of Jake's. So why would Gloria ask if James told me who killed them? It bothered me so much that I had to take the rest of the day off.

CHAPTER 1

I Know It Was The Blood

WHAT'S HAPPENING? WHY ARE THE POLICE COMING TO the house? Why is mommy running down the street with no shoes on? Why is Juanita hugging me saying, "Dawn, it's gonna be alright"? It had to be serious because my family usually called me by Nikki, my nickname, unless I was in trouble or they were having a serious conversation. What is she talking about? The worst of the day was over. We had already buried Pop-Pop. Why is everybody acting crazy all over again?

I was six years old when the worst week of my life happened. It started May 12th, 1976. I'll never forget it. My Nana had cooked my favorite dinner, fried chicken, mashed potatoes, and corn. I begged my mom to eat dinner there. Usually, she would pick me up after work, we would go home, and she would cook dinner. We lived a couple of blocks from my grandparents, Ernestine & Cecil. I really loved them. I spent a lot of time at their house. Mommy worked at the Electric Company and didn't get off in time to pick me up from school. Every

day after school, I took the school bus to my grandparents' house.

I loved going there after school and spending time with my Nana and Pop-Pop. I liked being around Mike and Pat too and their friends. Mike and Pat are really my aunt and uncle but felt more like my brother and sister because they were only ten and eleven years older than me. They knew all the latest fashion and music and would teach me all of the dances. They loved showing me off too. I could dance and their friends would be impressed with my moves. We lived in the house with them my entire life until mom married my stepdad, Henry. Everybody called him Hank. I liked him too, but I had a hard time moving to their house. They all called my mom Lil Cicely. She was named after her aunt and my Nana's sister. I was always with my Nana and if I wasn't with her, I was with my Pop-Pop.

After we ate dinner that night, we were sitting around talking and my Pop-Pop got up and went to bathroom because he said he had a stomachache. Everybody was laughing at Michael because he said that Judie Budie, some girl from the neighborhood, was messing around with Mr. Clark. Mr. Clark was around eighty-five years old at the time and lived across the street. He was a dirty old man and would always try to get me to sit on his lap when my Nana or Pop Pop wasn't looking. I fell for it the first time and he start humping on my butt. I never went near him after that.

Once they stopped laughing all loud, I heard Pop-Pop calling for Nana.

"Nana, Pop-Pop is in the bathroom and he's calling you."

She left the kitchen to go see what he wanted and she came running back in the kitchen yelling, "Call an ambulance! Cecil is having another heart attack!"

Everyone left the table to go to the bathroom to see what was going on. They were all blocking the door so it was hard for me to see him. I was trying to see through their legs and squeeze through. I needed to see his face! I heard the sirens from the ambulance as it got closer. When they finally got to the house, they came in with a stretcher. Everybody had to clear out of the hallway because it was so narrow, but I couldn't move. That's when I saw him sitting on the toilet and holding his chest. His pants were down around his ankles and he only had on a t-shirt. I guess he had gotten hot and taken off the shirt that he had on at dinner. When I looked at him, he didn't look good to me. He looked like the brown color had left his face and he had a gray, ashy look to his skin.

The paramedics rushed in and started asking him all kinds of questions. He was barely answering so my Nana was answering in between crying. I guess she knew it was bad too. They gave him smelling salt which I guess is supposed to wake you up but it didn't seem like it worked.

"He's not going to be able to get up, so we're going to have to get him on the stretcher," said one of the

paramedics. It took three of them to get him on the stretcher. Pop-Pop wasn't a little man. He was medium height and on the fat side.

Once they got him on the stretcher and put him in the ambulance, that was the last time I ever saw my Pop-Pop alive.

We all jumped in the cars and went to the hospital. I don't ever remember being that scared. When we got in the emergency room, they told us that he was in with the doctors. But after about ten minutes, a short, White, bald-headed man came out and very casually said, "He didn't make it."

I didn't know what that meant but everybody started screaming and hollering. My Nana fell to her knees, screaming. Mike and Pat were crying. My mommy was sitting in a chair with her hands over her face crying too. By now, Hank had come in and he picked me up and started hugging me.

"Daddy, why is everybody crying?"

"Pop-Pop is dead," he said.

I didn't know what was going on when he said that Pop-Pop was dead. What did that mean? This was the first time I ever heard that anyone I knew was dead. They kept saying, "He's never coming back!" I wanted to know what they meant.

The next day, I was so sad. I still didn't even understand why. I didn't realize that death was forever.

Apparently, my Pop-Pop wasn't coming back. Mike and Pat were sad too. They stayed in their room all day because it was so many people coming by the house. They didn't go to school all week and none of their friends came over. My mom didn't let me go to school either that week.

After a couple of nights had passed, a man named Carl Miller came by the house to talk to my Nana about the funeral arrangements. They talked for a long time. She signed a bunch of papers and my Nana gave him a new suit and shoes that she had gotten for Pop-Pop. I was really confused. Why did Pop-Pop need new clothes if he was dead? None of this made sense to me, probably because I had never been to a funeral before. Mr. Miller told my Nana that the family could come by to view the body the next day. Now I was more confused than before. View the body? What body were they talking about?

The next day when it was time to go, I noticed that everyone was getting sad when we were on our way. My mom told my Nana that she had a valium pill that would calm her nerves. Why did she need a pill to calm her nerves? My mom and dad told me to ride with them and Nana rode with my Uncle Butch. He was my favorite Uncle when he wasn't drunk and acting crazy.

As soon as I got in the car, my mom said, "Pawn Pawn?" That was her nickname for me. "We want to talk to you about what's going on."

They explained death and going to Heaven and being with the Lord. They told me about how Pop-Pop had died

and all about a funeral. They let me ask any questions that I had and I had a lot. They were very patient with me and we talked all the way to the funeral home.

When we pulled up, they explained that we were going to view Pop-Pop's body. They told me that his spirit had left to go be with the Lord and that the only thing that was left was his body.

"Dawn, there is nothing to be afraid of. The dead can't hurt you, only the living," said my dad. He picked me up and we went inside.

I had no idea what to expect. I was shaking! All I saw was a funny-looking bed that had a hard cover on the top. I later found out that it was called a casket. I heard my Nana saying that the casket they chose was really nice, top of the line. It was a shiny gray color and had a lot of flowers around it. The flowers were really pretty.

We must have been in the room about ten minutes when the man that came to the house came in. Everything was starting to make sense. There was a sign outside that said Carl Miller's Funeral Home. The funeral home was named after him so he must own it.

"Good evening family and friends, let us pray." He prayed for our family and for the Lord to bless and keep us during these trying times. Everybody had their eyes closed except for me, I was still too scared. Something didn't feel right. The casket just sitting there gave me a funny feeling. After he finished praying, he called for some of his men to come over and they started lifting the

top on the casket.

When they got it all the way open and I saw that my Pop-Pop was in there like he was sleeping, I screamed at the top of my lungs. My heart was beating a mile a minute and I was trembling uncontrollably.

"No, not my Pop-Pop!" He was really never coming back. Once I started screaming and crying, it seemed like my whole family broke down. Pop-Pop looked like he was sleeping except there was no snoring and he wasn't breathing. My dad got up and took me outside. I guess they had no idea that I would act like that. I didn't talk to anyone for the rest of the night.

I heard my Nana ask my Mom, "How is she going to be able to handle the funeral tomorrow?" My mom said, "I don't know but there's no one to watch her so she's gotta go." She told my Nana that she would talk to me and try to get me ready.

Even with what they had said, I didn't know what to expect. Everyone was at my Nana's house in the morning. All of my Nana's sisters were there along with my cousins. It was like a family reunion, the only person missing was Pop-Pop. Our church was only two minutes away from Nana and Pop-Pop's house so everyone lined up and started walking to the church. There were so many cars at the church that people were parked all down the street and into our driveway. As we were walking up to the church, there were still people going inside. The people that worked with Carl Miller made us wait until

everybody else went into the church. My dad was holding me when we walked inside but I was still shaking.

When the church doors opened, all I saw was the same casket from Carl Miller's Funeral Home sitting down front. Some people stood in front of the casket looking at my Pop-Pop. My dad knew not to take me up there so he didn't follow the family when they went to look at Pop-Pop. Instead, we went and sat in the pew.

Once all of the family was seated, they closed the casket. I was happy about that. I know that my dad said that the dead can't hurt you but they sure can scare you. Jamilla Woods sang the song, "The Blood That Jesus Shed For Me." I fell in love with the song and the words. For some reason, hearing the song and being in my dad's arms during the funeral was comforting.

After the funeral, all of the people came back to my house. They were everywhere. I was feeling a lot better and me and my cousins were running around playing. For a minute, my mind was off the fact that my Pop-Pop was never coming back. We played all day and all the grown-ups sat around talking. For the first time in a week, things seemed a little normal. It was starting to get dark and some people were starting to leave. They told my Nana that they would be back for the burial in the morning. I didn't really know what that meant but I liked having all the people around because it wasn't so sad.

Me and my cousins were in the room watching TV when we saw the police pull up in the driveway. We went

to the window to see what was going on but we couldn't hear what he was saying to my mom. Whatever he said made her take off running down the street. She didn't have on any shoes and nobody could catch her. I ran out of the room and everybody was crying all over again. I started crying and asking why was my mommy running down the street. That's when cousin Juanita grabbed me and started hugging me, saying that everything was going to be alright. I looked over at my Nana and she just stared into space. She looked like she wasn't really there. Mike and Pat were crying and all of the people that were at the house were crying too. What was going on? That's when I heard Uncle Walt say, "I can't believe that Hank is dead!"

CHAPTER 2

The Past Was Haunting Me

WHEN I LEFT WORK, I WENT STRAIGHT HOME. I KEPT asking God why now. It had been over a decade since anyone talked about the murder of James or Jake. Why did Gloria ask if James had told me who killed him? That was a crazy question in the first place because how can you be killed and telling who the killer is. But I knew what she meant. How did she know what she meant? That was the question that needed to be answered. Why is she back in town and why did she leave town in the first place? My mind raced all night. I finally fell asleep but when I woke up in the morning, I couldn't get Gloria off of my mind.

When I got to work in the morning, the first thing I saw on my desk was the application Gloria had filled out. Peter had taken most of the information before he brought her over to me. Right there on the application was her address where she wanted to get the phone service. She lived on 12th and Lehigh Avenue in North Philly, not too far my church. In the back of my mind, I wanted to go there and talk to her but that would put

me and my job in jeopardy so I quickly let that plan go. She said she would come back another time and when she did, I would be right there waiting for her. I made sure to tell all of the customer service agents that if a customer by the name of Gloria Peters came in, to send her to me.

Every day for over a month I waited for her to come back in. I even started to pack my lunch so I wouldn't be out on lunch break and miss her. She did not come back in! It was really bothering me because I needed to know what she meant by her question and more importantly that she didn't say this to anyone else. I had kept the address that she put on her application in my desk and something kept rising up in me to go to her house and ask her what she meant. Every day I waited for her to come in and every day that she didn't, I thought about going to her house.

It was killing me. One day after church, I decided that I was going to drive past that block on my way home. I guess I just wanted to see where she lived because I had no intention of going to her door. When I got to her block and was about to make the turn, something inside of me wouldn't let me do it. I thought about all of the trouble I could get in if she called my job and said that I was stalking her so I kept going straight down Broad Street and went home. I was going to get my questions answered but not at the risk of losing my job!

For the next month, I thought about all different kinds of ways to get to Gloria. I had lost contact with

all of the people that we knew when we were hanging at Jake's that may have known her. There had to be some way. That Sunday when I went to church, the sermon was about "Getting Closure." I was sure that this was a sign from God that I needed to get closure with Gloria. I made up in my mind that I was going to her house. If she was bold enough to ask me that question and mess my mind up for two months, I was bold enough to knock on her door and ask her what she meant. I had been with Bell Atlantic long enough for them to love and respect me that I could explain the situation if it came down to it. I couldn't wait for church to be over.

All the way there, I kept playing out the worst-case scenario. The way she was acting when she was at Bell Atlantic was like she was scared to death of me. What if she tried to kill me? That wasn't logical. What if she called the police? But what for? I hadn't done anything. So, I wiped my mind clear of all the what if's and just drove to her house. When I got there, I sat in the car for what seemed like an hour before I got up the courage to get out and go up to the door. The house was a cute, white row home with flowers planted in the front and a little white fence. I opened the fence and went up to the door and rang the bell. My heart was beating like an African drum. Somebody yelled, "Coming!" I heard the slippers dragging on the hardwood floors by whoever was coming to open the door. When the door flung open, it was Gloria. When she saw that it was me, she didn't look

as surprised as I thought she would. She was standing in her bathrobe and slippers and I think we were both in shock, so we just stood there looking at each other for what felt like eternity.

She finally said, "I knew you were coming, what took you so long?"

I was surprised. She opened the screen door to let me in and then she started walking to the back. I went in and closed the door behind me and followed her. She lit a cigarette and kept staring at me. I was standing there probably looking as crazy as I felt.

"Go ahead, have a seat," she said.

At least now she wasn't acting scared of me. I think the roles were reversed because I was scared to death. What am I doing in this lady's house and how did she know I was coming? It was weird that she'd asked about James and now she's saying that she knew I was coming.

"You have a real nice place," I said as I sat down.

"Stop with the bullsh*t and let's get right down to why you're here."

I was surprised at how forward she was so I said, "Okay, why did you ask me if James told me who killed him?"

"Because I wanted to know if he told you."

"What would make you ask me that kind of question?"

She looked at me and shook her head.

"You really watch too much TV," she said.

She walked to the cabinet and took out a bottle of vodka and asked me if I wanted a drink. I asked her what she meant by I watched too much TV.

"If you thought James could drive himself to your house in his condition then you've watched too many Robert Redford movies."

After she said that I asked for that shot of vodka.

Gloria started replaying the night that me and my sisters' lives changed forever. She started by saying that it had happened a long time ago and that she wasn't proud of a lot of the things she'd done back then. She took some time to get her life in order but that this always haunted her and she was glad she was finally able to get it off of her chest.

Apparently, when Gloria worked for Sugie, she was also one of Jake's girls and he had plenty of them. When everyone left that night, she and Jake left James at the bar and he was real drunk. She said her and Jake went in the back to get it on like they did every Saturday night after he closed up. He was sitting at his desk and Gloria was on her knees sucking his d**k when they heard Bea come in.

She heard Bea say, "You think you're the boss and you can embarrass me in front of all those people motherf**cker?" She said she never heard James say a word before she heard gunshots. Jake jumped up and pulled his pants up and went to see what was going on but before he could get out of his office, Bea was in there pointing a gun at him. Gloria said she hid under the desk

because she knew if she moved, Bea would kill her too.

Then Bea said, "Jake, I'm sorry that I have to involve you in this but I'm going to need you to open the safe and give me the money."

Jake was real calm and said, "Bea, you don't have to do this. We're like family."

Bea said, "We're not family!" Gloria said Bea was laughing as she said, "Do you see what I just did to the closest person to me that was like family?" She told Jake again to open the safe.

While Jake was opening the safe, he said, "If you need money Bea, I'll give it to you. You don't have to go about it like this." Bea told him to shut the f**k up and just open the safe. Gloria said Jake asked her to stop pointing the gun at his head before it accidentally went off. Jake must have been taking too long to open the safe so Bea hit him with the gun. She told him that she wasn't playing with him and he had five seconds to open it.

Gloria finally heard Jake say, "Here! Take the money just don't kill…," but before he could get the word out, the gun went off and Gloria saw Jake's brains splatter all over the wall. Gloria heard Bea laugh and say, "This white motherf**ker thought he was going to come into the community and make all the money off of us," as she threw the money in a bag.

Gloria told me she had never been so scared in all of her life. She waited until Bea left and she heard the door close before she finally came out. When she came

from underneath the desk, she saw Jake's lifeless body lying there with a hole in the side of his head and blood and brain tissue everywhere. She ran to the trash can and started throwing up. She knew he was dead. She grabbed all of her stuff and was about to leave out the back door but it was chained with a lock on it so she had to go out front. As she ran to the front door, she heard James moaning. She said that she wanted to get the heck out of there but something made her go over to him. She was scared to death because she didn't know if Bea would come back or if someone would walk in and think that she had shot them or set them up to be shot.

When she went to check on James, he was breathing. All the alcohol must have helped him survive the shots to his abdomen and chest. She said she leaned down and helped him to sit up. He kept saying, "Please get my key out of my pocket. Get my car and take me to 4907 Cedar Avenue." Gloria told him she was scared and just wanted to call the ambulance and leave. He grabbed her arm and begged her to get his key and his car and drive him to 4907 Cedar Avenue. He promised her that the killer would not come back to the scene of the crime for fear of getting caught. Gloria was scared that Bea was still outside and would see her coming out of Jake's and kill her too. James said that in his right pocket were his keys, his car was the Thunderbird parked right outside and that in his left pocket was $200 that she was to take for herself.

She said she went to the window to see if anybody

was outside but it was 3:20am so the streets were empty. She went outside and unlocked the car and then went back in and helped James outside. She had never driven such a big car so she was scared of that, scared that somebody would see her and even more scared of getting pulled over by the police. James was not looking so good on the ride and there was blood everywhere. When she finally reached the address, he asked her to help him to the door. She said that he was very weak at that point but she managed to get him to the house and leaned him up on the door. There were no parking spaces available in the front of my house so she just parked in the middle of the street. She rang the doorbell a lot of times and was waiting for the lights to come on. She was scared out of her mind so she kept ringing the bell and went across the street to wait for someone to answer the door so she could leave. When she finally saw me open the door and knew that it was my house that he had asked her to bring him to, she felt a sense of relief. Everybody knew that James and I were together for years.

Gloria said it was like she was in a trance and couldn't move for about ten minutes. She couldn't believe what had happened. She had no idea how she was getting home because she lived in North Philly. Just as she was about to move James' car, she started hearing police sirens. But before the police arrived, she saw a car coming down my block. She was so scared to see a car coming down the block at that time of morning, she ducked behind a

parked car. When she saw that it was Bea, she panicked! She thought Bea knew that she had brought James to my house. She said that Bea parked down the block and waited for the police to get there. After the police had been inside for five minutes, that's when Bea came to the door. Gloria left Philly the next morning with the money James had given her and the keys to his car. She was so scared that she had actually taken the keys by accident but that she was too frightened to bring them back. She threw them in a dumpster.

It all made sense because we never could find the keys to his car. The night that James died, Walter went to move his car and he couldn't find the keys. In fact, we never found the keys. The police had the car towed to the station. Gloria had moved back to Philly because her mother had recently passed and she wanted to be closer to her family. She hadn't even been in town for a week and hadn't seen anyone from the past in ten years until she saw me at the phone company. Momma used to always say that everything that happens in the dark will eventually come to light.